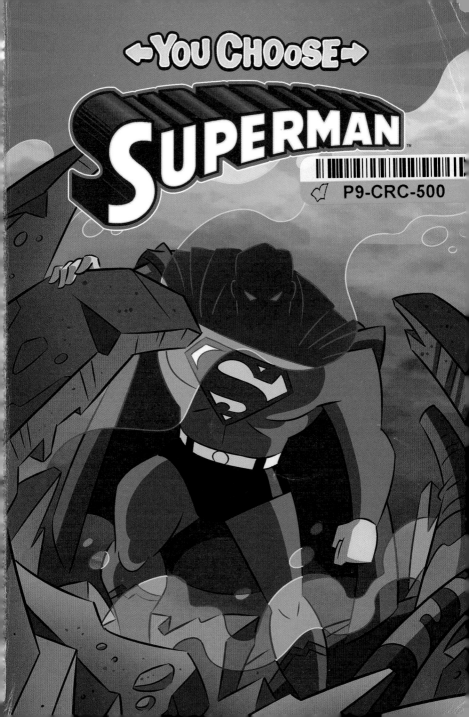

←YOU CHOOSE→

SUPERMAN™

P9-CRC-500

You Choose Stories: Superman
is published by Stone Arch Books,
A Capstone Imprint
1710 Roe Crest Drive
North Mankato, Minnesota 56003
www.mycapstone.com

STAR39714

Cataloging-in-Publication Data is available
on the Library of Congress website.
ISBN: 978-1-4965-5827-5 (library binding)
ISBN: 978-1-4965-5832-9 (paperback)
ISBN: 978-1-4965-5838-1 (eBook)

Summary: Lex Luthor is up to his old tricks. He's got
a secret plan to deceive Metropolis and defeat Superman
at the same time. It's up to Superman to find out what's
really going on and save the people of Metropolis.
Only you can help the Man of Steel put a stop to
Lex Luthor's devious schemes!

Printed in the United States of America.
010830S18

YOU CHOOSE

SUPERMAN™

METROPOLIS MAYHEM

Superman created by
Jerry Siegel and Joe Shuster
by special arrangement with the Jerry Siegel Family

written by
Sarah Hines Stephens

illustrated by
Dario Brizuela

STONE ARCH BOOKS
a capstone imprint

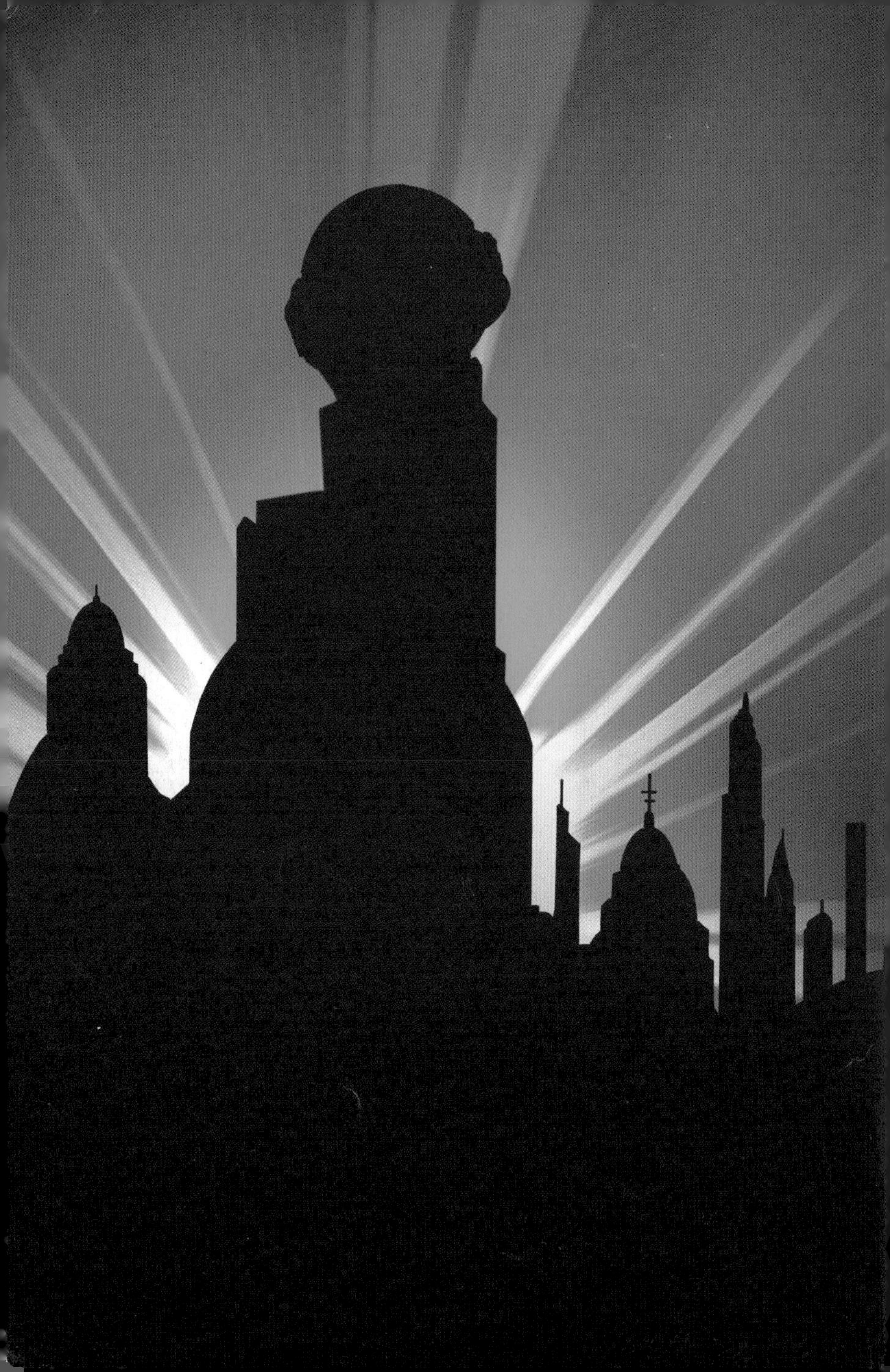

Crafty businessman and criminal mastermind
Lex Luthor has a new plan in place to defeat
Superman. But his plans also call for deceiving the
people of Metropolis and putting them in serious
danger. Only YOU can help stop him. With your
help, the Man of Steel can defeat Lex's dangerous
schemes in *Metropolis Mayhem*!

Follow the directions at the bottom of each page.
The choices YOU make will change the outcome
of the story. After you finish one path, go back and
read the others for more Superman adventures!

Metropolis is buzzing like a hive of bees. The city is usually crowded, but today it is beyond busy. Thousands of people fill the streets. Traffic is at a near standstill, and helicopters whirl above it all. People have arrived from all over the world in order to attend the first ever LEX-CON. The big convention is the brainchild of billionaire businessman Lex Luthor. Everyone is eager to see what he has in store inside the city's Convention Center.

LexCorp has been hyping the convention for months. LEX-CON banners hang from every light post on Main Street. Enormous LEX-CON billboards tower over the highways. Each one features a large image of a smiling Lex Luthor proudly proclaiming, *LEX-CON: The Future is Here!*

"Luthor's going all out. He wants everyone to know about his circus," reporter Clark Kent tells Lois Lane and Jimmy Olsen, the *Daily Planet* team.

Turn the page.

Lois Lane agrees. She's covering the convention with Clark, but they're not the only reporters. There are news teams from all over.

"Luthor does like a crowd," Lois replies. "But can he deliver?"

"Lex has been bragging for weeks," Clark says. "He claims he and his highly paid *Innovention* team have created devices that will change the future, and the world."

Luthor's claims almost make Clark laugh — but the savvy reporter knows better than to underestimate Luthor. The man has unlimited resources and a devious mind. He has surprised Clark more than once.

Clark suspects the real purpose of LEX-CON is not innovation. It's about promoting the man behind the show. But suspicions don't make good news stories — truth and facts do. And Clark is eager to find the truth and give his readers the real facts.

Finally the convention center doors open and everyone is allowed inside. Clark lets himself be swept along with the crowd. Lois and Jimmy are with him. Cameras flash everywhere.

All around them Luthor's showy devices are impressively displayed. Lab techs stand nearby wearing white coats, eager to explain how each device works.

There's so much to see that Clark isn't sure where to begin. But then a large sparkling case on one side of the huge room catches his attention. He motions for Lois and Jimmy to follow.

"That's Lex's battle suit!" Jimmy exclaims when they get closer.

"*New and improved* battle suit," the lab tech says, overhearing him. "This specially designed battle armor has been completely upgraded and now includes a remote control." She holds the remote like a trophy.

Turn the page.

Why would Luthor need to control his armor from the outside? Clark wonders. He steps forward to take a closer look. At that same moment Lois takes his arm.

"Clark, look." Lois directs his attention toward a huge curtained stage at the back of the room. Spotlights swirl across the heavy drapes as they are dramatically pulled aside. Behind them a fleet of shiny humanoid robots stand in orderly rows.

"In the future, no home or business will be without a LexClean 8000," another Innovention Technician announces. "These domestic robots will soon be more common than vacuum cleaners. And they can do much more than just clean your home. All courtesy of LexCorp!"

Clark and Lois exchange looks. Things that sound too good to be true usually are.

Suddenly the lights dim. A voice booms over the loudspeakers. Spotlights focus in the center of the room. "Ladies and gentleman, put your hands together for the founder of LEX-CON and the creator of the future — Lex Luthor!"

A stage rises from the floor, lifting Luthor to meet the crowd.

"Welcome to LEX-CON!" Luthor gestures grandly around the room. "These are my gifts to you and to the world. They'll help make your lives easier and help protect the Earth.

"I hope you enjoy all of the "innoventions" here in this room. But there is another so grand it can only be demonstrated outside. I'll be exhibiting the LexSphere on the roof. Please, come and witness for yourselves the future in defense technology."

"Promises, promises," Clark says. Luthor is always boasting.

If Clark goes to get a closer look at the battle suit, turn to page 13.

If Clark checks out the LexCleans with Lois, turn to page 15.

If Clark heads to the roof to see the LexSphere, turn to page 17.

THE ULTIMATE DEFENSE
AGAINST INTERFERING
ALIENS

While some of the crowd heads for the roof, Clark goes the other way. He wants a closer look at the battle suit. It has features like super-strength, durability, and flight to match Superman's powers. Luthor claims the suit was created to help protect the people of Earth. But Clark knows its true intention — to destroy Superman!

It's no secret Luthor hates the Man of Steel. He has tried to destroy Superman before. By wearing the suit, he's come frighteningly close. Clark knows that, sooner or later, Superman will have to battle the big shot bully in his improved suit. The more he can find out about the suit's upgrades and improvements the better.

The purple and green suit gleams in the case. Below it a sign proclaims it to be: The Ultimate Defense Against Interfering Aliens.

That's ironic, Clark thinks with a frown, *since it's alien-made*.

Turn the page.

Clark lowers his glasses. He tries to see inside the suit using his X-ray vision. It's no use. The case is made from leaded glass. Clark suspects that the suit is lined with Kryptonite. Just being near the suit would weaken Superman. It's also armed with Kryptonite-fueled weapons, including energy blasts and plasma blades.

"Can you tell us what's different about this suit?" Clark asks the tech who is showing off the armor.

"I can do better than that," the technician says. He holds up a remote and pushes a button. Clark winces as the case opens and the suit slowly rises into the air. "I can show you! Follow me, everyone," the tech tells the audience. Then he guides the battle suit and the onlookers toward the exit doors.

Clark feels unsteady. The Kryptonite in the suit is making him feel strange. And he has a bad feeling that something is about to go terribly wrong!

If Clark stays to watch the battle suit demonstration, turn to page 19.

If Clark changes into Superman to deal with the suit, turn to page 26.

Luthor's stage sinks into the floor while the crowd cheers. Lois rolls her eyes. "He sure likes to hear applause."

"Yes, almost as much as he likes money," Clark agrees.

Lois appears lost in thought. "You're right, Clark. Luthor does love money. But didn't he say he was giving these robots away? Why would he do that?" Lois makes a beeline for the LexClean stage to find the answer for herself.

Clark waves for Jimmy and they both follow. Lois could be on to something!

On the LexClean stage the techs are making a mess.

"Oops!" One tech pretends to spill a box of cereal.

"Oh no!" the other says, splattering milk all over the stage.

One of the LexCleans whirs into action. It scoops up the mess, wipes the floor clean, and dries it.

Turn the page.

"Who wouldn't want a LexClean in their home?" the tech asks. The crowd applauds.

"And here's the best part," the other tech adds. "Lex Luthor will be providing these robots to every home, apartment, and office in Metropolis — free of charge!"

The audience goes wild.

"Lois Lane, *Daily Planet*!" Lois shouts over the noise. "Why would Lex Luthor give away something that people would be willing to buy?" she asks.

"Lex Luthor is a visionary," the tech replies. "He's putting his concern for the cleanliness of our city ahead of profits. He hopes to eliminate common illnesses and increase people's health and productivity! That's why we'll begin giving away all of the LexCleans you see here on stage, today!"

More techs in lab coats circulate, taking names for the giveaway drawing. On stage the name of the first winner is announced. A man in the crowd hoots and rushes up to collect his prize.

If Clark follows the man and his LexClean robot, turn to page 22.
If Clark sneaks away to become Superman, turn to page 28.

Most of the people head for the elevators. They're anxious to see what Luthor has to show them on the roof. Lois excuses herself to get a closer look at the LexCleans. Jimmy goes with her, but Clark follows the crowd. He is curious about the LexSphere.

When he reaches the rooftop the crowd is already thick. Clark tries to make his way to the front. Before he can get there a dozen drones are launched into the air. The drones fly up and hover overhead. Then Lex Luthor's voice booms through giant speakers, "Citizens of Metropolis, I give you — LexSphere!"

Clark removes his glasses and holds up a hand, pretending to shield his eyes from the sun. Using his X-ray vision, he scans one of the drones. He sees it has some sort of electronic devices attached to a lead-lined unit, but he cannot see through the lead.

Turn the page.

"Ladies and gentlemen, with the push of a button you'll be safer than you've ever been on planet Earth," Lex says, gesturing grandly. "My LexSphere creates a floating, dome-shaped shield that can protect us from any attack! We never know when unfriendly aliens might appear." Luthor scans the crowd looking for something . . . or someone.

Clark ducks his head, avoiding Luthor's gaze. Aliens . . . external attack . . . it sounds to Clark like Luthor is talking about Superman!

Luthor's finger presses a button on a remote control while Clark looks for a place to change. As Lex peers out at the crowd a smile spreads across his face. "Once I've activated the LexSphere, I have another surprise in store — a live demonstration! That's right, I've arranged a little friendly missile fire. It's headed our way now, so you can see for yourselves how strong the LexSphere is!" The crowd rumbles in alarm. "Please don't panic!" Luthor chuckles. "You're all perfectly safe."

If Clark slips away to change into Superman, turn to page 24.
If Clark stays to see the LexSphere in action, turn to page 30.

As the crowd gathers outside, Clark staggers and raises his hand to his forehead. The green Kryptonite in the battle suit is giving him a massive headache. And then his suspicions are confirmed when the tech makes an announcement. In order to demonstrate the suit properly, they're going to stage a mock battle!

Luthor is trying to draw me out, Clark thinks. *He wants Superman to fight against the battle suit here and now! But I'm not taking the bait.*

The lights flicker and a strangely familiar voice booms over the speakers. "All right, let's show these gawkers exactly what Luthor means by an 'upgrade' . . ."

Clark knows that voice. It sounds just like Metropolis radio shock jock Leslie Willis! Willis used to enjoy dragging Superman's name through the mud on air. But when she lost her job and was struck by lightning, she was forever changed . . .

Turn the page.

. . . into Livewire!

The electrified villain reveals herself, emerging from a nearby electrical light. Her blue spiked hair crackles with energy.

The crowd begins to buzz nervously. "Are they going to fight?" one person asks.

"Right here? That doesn't seem very safe," another states.

Livewire flies closer to the suit, circling. The tech controlling the headless armor keeps it at a distance. Tiny blue bolts of electricity spark between Livewire's fingers. The tech pushes a button on the remote and one of the suit's armored hands pulses with green light.

Clark winces. He looks around for something to protect the people. He wants to stop the madness unfolding before him. He spots a nearby tank of water where submersible drones are being demonstrated. Behind that is a garbage dumpster.

If Clark tries to short-circuit Livewire, turn to page 33.

If Clark changes into Superman to stop the battle suit, turn to page 49.

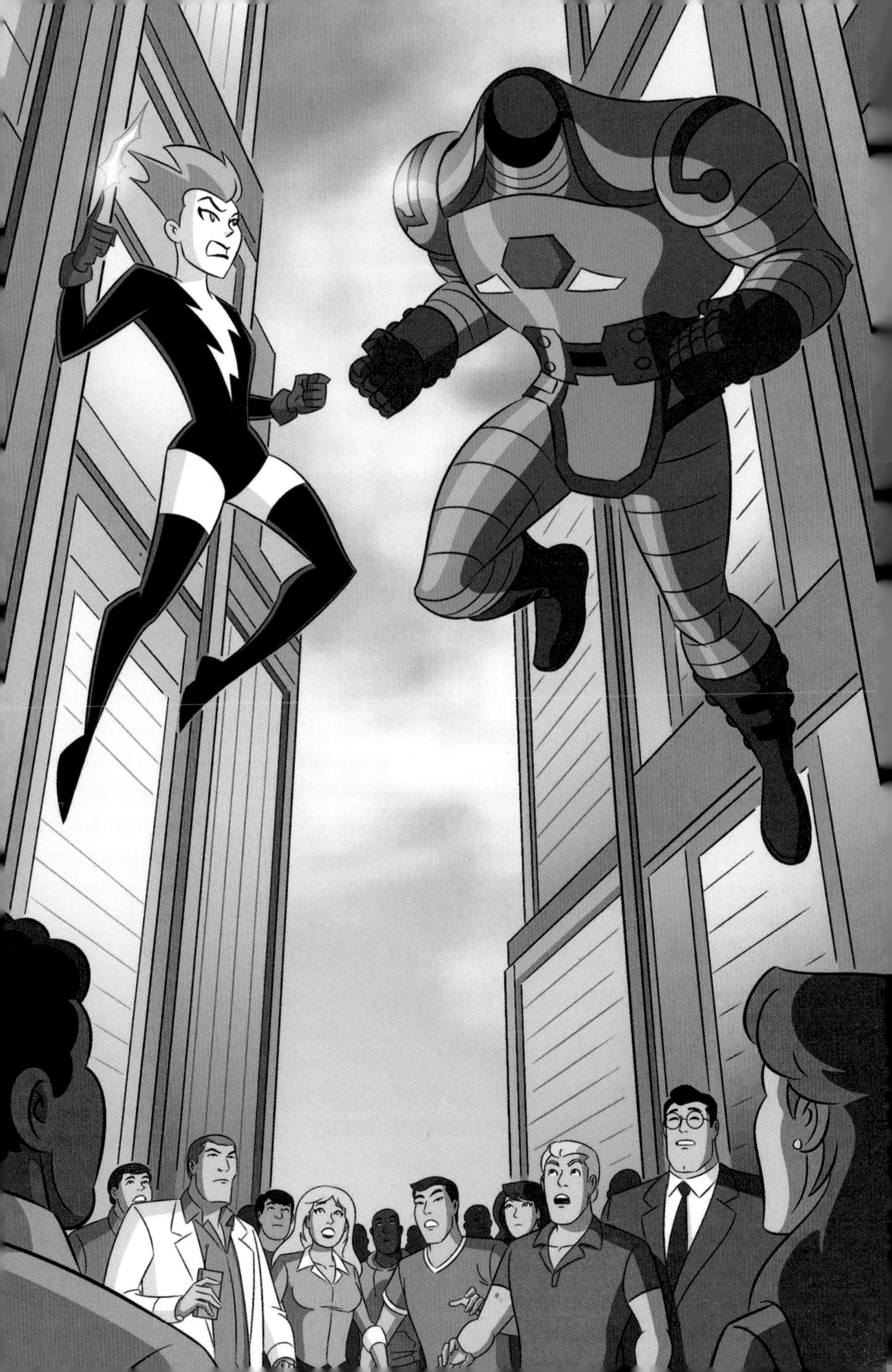

Clark watches the winner, a man in a brown suit, collect his prized LexClean robot. The lab tech instructs the man to look into the robot's eye — a glass panel on the front of its head.

"Once your LexClean has imprinted on you, it's yours for life," the tech tells him. The man leans in so the LexClean can scan his face. When he moves away, the LexClean follows him like a loyal dog.

Dozens of LexCleans wait behind the technician. Soon dozens of new owners are lined up to collect them.

Clark follows the first winner as he moves around the hall. As the man looks at various displays, his LexClean stays close. The robot doesn't do anything unusual, but Clark still feels there's something fishy about the whole situation. As the number of LexCleans roaming the convention floor grows, so does Clark's unease.

Clark is about to ask the man if he can take a closer look at his prize when the man heads for the exit. The LexClean follows him outside, with Clark just a few paces behind.

Though he's dressed like Clark Kent, Superman's senses are on high alert. As soon as they exit the building he hears something strange. Radio waves outside the range of human hearing are coming from the LexClean. The robot is sending out some sort of coded communication. But why would a cleaning robot have a transmitter?

Clark lowers his glasses to use his X-ray vision, but the LexClean has a lead lining. He can't see a thing.

Clark reaches for his phone to call Lois. "You were right," he says when she answers. "There's more to these 'cleaning robots' than meets the eye."

If Clark tries to open a LexClean to look inside, turn to page 35.

If he tries to learn the information that the LexClean is sending, turn to page 52.

Slipping out of the nervous crowd, Clark ducks into the empty stairwell to change. He can't believe how reckless Luthor is being! There's no way that the self-proclaimed 'protector' of Metropolis has tested his LexSphere against missile fire. If LexCorp was doing serious weapons testing, Clark would have heard about it — or Superman would have sensed it. Either way, he would know. Testing the shield here and now is putting hundreds, if not thousands, of people in danger!

Luckily stopping a few missiles is an easy task for the Man of Steel.

Superman emerges into the sunlight — the very thing that gives him his powers. At that same moment Luthor pushes a button to activate the LexSphere. The drones beam reddish light from their sides. The flat planes connect with light from other drones. Together they form a glowing dome over several city blocks.

Inside the dome the light is altered. Everything has taken on a reddish color.

Superman feels strange as he prepares to fly through the LexSphere to stop the incoming missiles.

Meanwhile, Luthor continues to brag. "Did anyone forget to wear sunscreen?" he asks the crowd. "Don't worry! The LexSphere works as sunscreen to block out the sun's harmful rays!"

Superman suddenly understands his wooziness. Luthor has cut him off from his source of power — the Earth's yellow sun! His solar-fueled strength is waning. Until he gets out of the red dome, he'll be as weak as any human being.

If Superman tries to get Luthor's controller, turn to page 37.

If Superman tries to fly through the LexSphere, turn to page 55.

Clark pushes his glasses up on his nose, and angles his hat to hide his face. He needs to find a place to change — fast! He spots a large tank filled with submersible drones. But it's not big enough for him to hide behind. And the lines for the restrooms in the crowded building are ridiculous. Finally Clark spots a sign for the fire exit . . . the stairwell will have to do.

"Excuse me. Pardon me." With his head throbbing from the Kryptonite-powered battle suit overhead, Clark makes his way to the exit.

The door closes and Clark changes quickly.

This is what Luthor wanted, Superman thinks. *He wanted me to show up and fight his battle suit. He was hoping for a public battle.*

Luthor is constantly complaining that Superman has selfish motives. He insists on pointing out how Superman is an alien and that he isn't to be trusted. Lex's comments remind Superman of the things radio shock jock Leslie Willis used to say about him before becoming Livewire.

Suddenly there is a surge in the lights. A voice erupts from the speakers. Livewire herself is addressing the crowd!

The former DJ loves a listening audience. She works the room to her advantage, asking how people are enjoying LEX-CON and prompting cheers. Then she announces that she's there to assist with one of Luthor's demos. "That's right everyone — I'm here to zap Luthor's battle suit!"

If Superman takes on Livewire, turn to page 68.
If Superman takes out the battle suit, turn to page 84.

While the technicians give away more LexCleans, Clark slips behind the curtain on the stage. When he emerges he is transformed!

"Superman!" Lois exclaims. "I didn't expect to see you at LEX-CON!"

Superman smiles at his favorite reporter. "I'm sure I would have enjoyed reading about all of this later. But I thought it might be better for me to see what Lex is up to personally. It's pretty strange for him to just give away these robots for free."

"You're telling me," Lois agrees. "And I don't think it's because he's worried about cleanliness!"

Lois and Superman look around the large room. Several dozen LexCleans are following their new owners. With his super-hearing the Man of Steel can tell they're sending wireless radio signals. But he can't decipher the information that they're sending.

"I need to get a closer look at one of these LexCleans," Superman tells Lois.

The reporter is already one step ahead of him. She dumps what's left of her coffee on the floor and exclaims loudly, "Oh no, what a mess!"

Immediately a LexClean arrives on the scene and begins to mop up the spill. "I am LexClean 524," the robot introduces itself. It hasn't been assigned to an owner yet.

Superman tries to use his X-ray vision to see inside the robot as it works. But the robot's body is lined with lead.

"Do you mind if I just . . ." Superman reaches for the robot, hoping to open the panel on its back and check the settings. But as soon as Superman touches the control panel, the robot freezes in place and begins blasting an alarm.

VRONK! VRONK! VRONK!

If Superman takes the panel off of the LexClean, turn to page 70.

If he tries to learn where the robot is sending its information, turn to page 88.

Clark is jostled by the worried crowd, and feels a bit worried himself. *What if Luthor's shield doesn't work the way he says it will? And what is this LexSphere made of anyway?* he wonders.

He doesn't have to wait long to find out. Luthor pushes a button to activate the LexSphere. The drones, all hovering in position, project beams of reddish light from each of their sides. The flat planes of red light connect with the light projected from the other drones to form a giant dome. The glowing red dome covers several city blocks.

Turn to page 32.

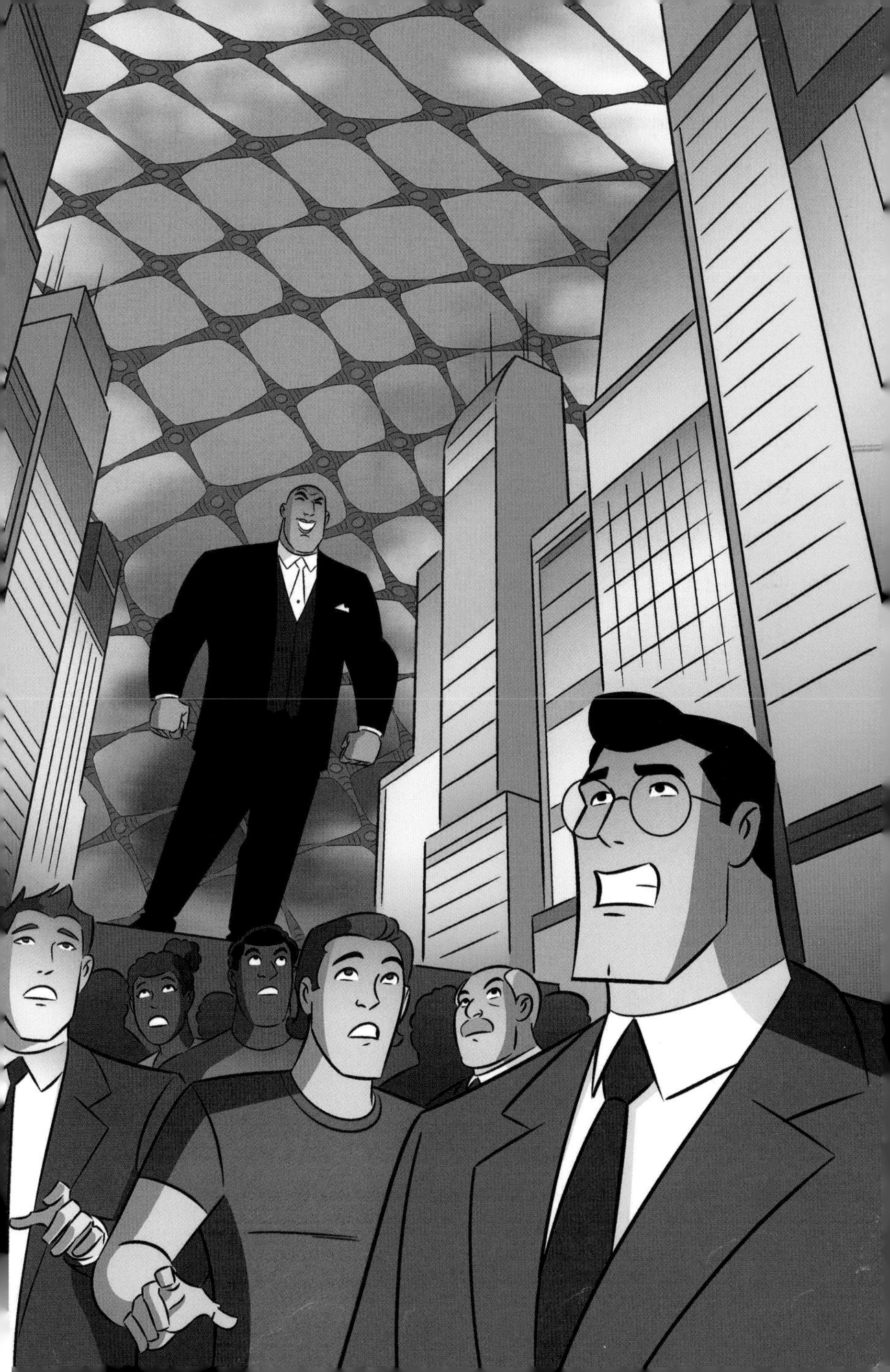

Beneath the dome everything looks red, and Clark feels strange. Luthor's shield is blocking the solar energy of Earth's yellow sun, the thing that gives Superman his powers. Even worse, it's draining his strength by imitating the red sun of Krypton!

Clark feels his powers fading. It won't be long before he is as weak as any Earthling. He was counting on his powers to protect the LEX-CON attendees and Metropolis from Luthor's missile test.

Squinting up at the LexSphere, Clark tries to guess how much of his power remains. Is it enough to knock out Luthor's shield? He would only need to take out a few drones to bring down the whole LexSphere. But he would have to get closer to the red Kryptonite light to do it.

If I can't knock out those missiles, maybe something else can, Clark thinks. *Something built for battle — like Luthor's battle suit!*

If Clark changes into Superman to take out the LexSphere, turn to page 72.

If Clark uses the battle suit to stop the missiles, turn to page 91.

Clark's head continues pounding with a severe headache. His arms and legs feel heavy. Keeping an eye on the enemies overhead, he backs toward the tank of submersible drones. He ducks behind it. The presence of the Kryptonite makes it hard to think. But he has to find a way to lure Livewire toward the water.

CRACK! Livewire discharges a bolt of electrical energy at the battle suit. Sparks rain down on the crowd below.

Clark sees the light and hears the screams. But the battle suit seems unharmed.

The lab tech smiles gleefully, and pushes buttons on the remote. The battle suit flies in circles around Livewire, its armored hands glowing green. Then it releases a plasma blast that surrounds Livewire in a cloud of Kryptonite energy. She's trapped! But not for long. Within seconds, she blasts the cloud away.

Clark winces. Livewire is unaffected by Kryptonite, but the plasma would have drained Superman's strength.

Turn the page.

Livewire prepares for her next attack. Clark can feel the electricity building. But he doesn't take his eyes off of the tech controlling the suit.

Lightning flashes. Livewire has unleashed another super-charged blast. This time a few pieces of the battle suit are blown off. Bits of hot metal fall into the screaming crowd. In the chaos Clark sees his opportunity. He sprints toward the tech and runs clumsily into him. Clark swipes at the tech's arm as he makes contact. The tech loses his grip on the remote control. It clatters to the ground and is lost in the crowd.

"No!" the tech shouts. The battle suit hovers motionless in the air and the green glow fades.

Livewire cackles. She rubs her hands together and gets ready to unleash her biggest blast on the unprotected armor.

Clark has no time to lose. He dives into the sea of feet. He has to get that remote control!

Turn to page 39.

"I need to see inside one of those robots," Clark tells Lois over the phone. But he first has to figure out how to get one away from its owner.

Stepping back inside the convention hall, Clark scans the scene. The place is crawling with LexCleans! Each robot is standing close to its new owner. Clark isn't sure how he can look inside one without calling attention to himself.

Suddenly he hears a familiar voice whoop in excitement.

"Woo hoo!" Jimmy Olsen is dancing around a brand new LexClean. "I'll never have to vacuum my floor again!"

Clark makes his way over and claps Jimmy on the back. "Congratulations, Jimmy!"

Jimmy grins. "Maybe I should take your picture!" Clark suggests. He snaps a few shots of Jimmy with his new robot, then asks the hard question. "Say, Jimmy, would you mind if I took a look inside of your LexClean?"

Jimmy shrugs. "Sure," he agrees.

Turn the page.

He and Clark move around to the back of the robot. There is a large panel with a warning on it in bright red:

STOP! DO NOT REMOVE.
FOR MAINTENANCE, PLEASE RETURN
TO LEXCORP.

Jimmy looks unsure, but Clark has to see inside! He wants to know if what he suspects is true — that the LexCleans' true purpose isn't as squeaky clean as it seems. He reaches for the panel and tries to pry it free. It doesn't budge. He'll have to use his super-strength.

"Jimmy, have you seen Lois?" Clark asks to distract him. When Jimmy turns to look for Lois, Clark removes the panel easily, but . . .

VRONK! VRONK! VRONK!

The LexClean starts blasting an ear-splitting alarm! The people in the center cover their ears and turn to see what's causing the noise.

Turn to page 42.

"In a few moments you'll hear the missiles approaching," Luthor announces.

Superman hears the nervous chatter of the crowd, but can't hear the missiles. With his super-hearing he can normally detect sounds as soft as the footstep of an ant in the Amazon. His powers are already waning. He has to act fast!

If I can get my hands on the LexSphere controller I can deactivate the shield, Superman thinks. *Then I could fly up to stop the missiles.*

The red light of the LexSphere dome changes the colors of everything under it. Superman's bright blue suit and red cape don't stand out as they usually do. He manages to slip behind the crowd.

He is just a few feet away from Luthor's podium when the bald man turns around. A huge smile spreads across Lex's face.

"Well look who's here," Luthor chuckles. "I knew you wouldn't be able to stay away, Superman!"

Turn the page.

"How could I stay away? You're risking people's lives!" Superman lunges for the LexSphere controller.

Luthor dodges. Superman stumbles. He's not used to his weakened state.

"People of Metropolis, this is the alien threat I'm trying to protect you from," Luthor points at Superman. "This monster is not from Earth. His planet was destroyed. Now he's trying to destroy ours. He wants to deactivate the LexSphere — the only thing keeping you safe!"

"Don't listen to him!" Superman shouts. "I'm trying to save you from those missiles!"

The people don't know what to believe or who to trust.

Superman moves toward Luthor. But a dozen people move to cut him off. He doesn't want to hurt anyone, but it looks like he is threatening the crowd!

Panic spreads like wildfire.

"Superman's gone crazy!" someone shouts.

Turn to page 45.

Clark slides to a stop and peers through the sea of legs. The remote is just beyond his reach. He crawls forward but the remote is kicked away. It spins across the sidewalk, stopping near the tech who is also frantically searching for it. Clark stands and pushes his way through the crowd.

The electric feeling is in the air once more. Overhead, Livewire laughs. "Looks like Luthor's new outfit isn't quite as unstoppable as he thought," she giggles. "Let's see if it can take this!"

Clark throws himself onto the remote as Livewire creates a blue arc of electricity between her palms.

Clark starts pushing buttons. His fingers move so fast they become a blur. Within seconds, the battle suit flies toward the ceiling.

Livewire discharges her blast. The charge misses the suit and hits the ceiling. Singed tiles rain down on the crowd.

Turn the page.

Livewire discharges bolt after bolt of blue lightning. Using the remote, Clark moves the suit out of the way each time. Livewire grows angrier by the moment.

Clark needs to shut the electric lady down before someone gets hurt. He punches buttons frantically. He has a plan, but for it to work he must fly the suit close to the crowd. It's a dangerous risk.

The crowd gasps as the battle suit turns and rockets toward them.

"That suit needs a recharge!" Livewire snarls. She unleashes a crackling bolt of electrical lightning while Clark guides the battle suit toward the water tank. It looks like the armor is about to take a hit. But at the last moment the suit swoops up, and the lightning arcs into the water!

With a powerful **POP!** every electrical circuit in the area is blown. The buildings go dark and Livewire is blasted back.

"Light's out, Livewire," Clark says to himself. The short-circuited villain slumps against the wall while Clark flies the suit back into its case. As soon as the battle suit is back behind the leaded glass Clark begins to feel like himself.

Soon the crowd is instructed to evacuate the area. LEX-CON has been cancelled.

Lois and Jimmy find Clark by the water tank.

"Well, I guess we got our story," Clark says. He smiles and pushes his glasses higher on his nose. The three start to leave, but the tech that had been operating the battle suit yells at Clark to stop.

"Give me back that remote," he yells.

"Oh, this? No problem." Clark walks toward the tech holding the controller out ahead of him.

"Oops!" he suddenly stumbles. The remote flies out of his hand and lands in the drone tank.

SPLASH!

THE END

To follow another path, turn to page 11.

Clark shrugs sheepishly and tries to find a way to silence the deafening alarm. Several of the Innovention Technicians are heading his way. But worse, Clark can hear high-frequency radio signals bouncing all over the building. Jimmy's LexClean is calling to the other robots — and they're responding!

Clark reaches into the back of Jimmy's robot and crushes the transmitter with his hand. The radio signals stop, but it's already too late. Every LexClean in the building knows his location. They are locked on and coming toward him. With so many people watching him, there's no way for Clark to change into Superman to meet the approaching threat! He has to find another way to knock out the robot fleet.

Clark quickly sends Lois a text message: *The LexCleans are communicating with each other. We need to find the central control and shut them down.*

As soon as the message is sent Clark is surrounded by LexCleans. He tries to shove them away, but without using his super-strength the machines are too strong.

Jimmy tries to stop them, but the LexCleans ignore him and press closer to Clark. Not even the techs seem to know what to do!

When there are so many robots that the crowd can't see him, Clark tears the back panel off of the closest one. The alarm sounds, and the LexClean sends out a radio signal. Clark rips out a handful of the robot's inner workings and it goes silent. But when he tries to disable another LexClean he yanks his hand back. The access panel is red hot — it's some sort of secret defense. The previous LexClean warned the others!

Clark kicks and pushes the LexCleans away.

Turn the page.

Finally he hears a familiar voice — Lex Luthor's. "Deactivate!" he shouts and the LexCleans freeze in their tracks.

Clark climbs out of the swarm of metal bodies. He sees Lex standing nearby with his arms crossed and a smug smile on his face.

"Mr. Kent. Did you find what you need? Do you have a good story for the *Daily Planet*?" Lex asks.

Clark pushes up his glasses. "Well, uh, Mr. Luthor, it sure looks like you have a few bugs to work out," he says with a forced laugh.

"On the contrary," Lex insists. "You just stumbled upon one of the LexClean upgrades I've been working on — personal protection services."

The crowd mumbles approval, but Clark just shakes his head. He knows that Luthor's LexCleans are designed to serve Luthor in some way. They might be an army, or a spy fleet . . . or something even more sinister. But he won't get the chance to prove that today.

THE END

To follow another path, turn to page 11.

Several people rush for the elevators.

Superman feels himself growing weaker. He can't fight his way through the crowd. And he doesn't trust that he has enough strength to fly. But he has an idea. He can use Luthor's own tools against him! He rides the elevator down with the crowd.

Superman rushes toward the technician getting ready to demonstrate the battle suit. He grabs the remote before the tech can react.

"I'll be taking this," Superman says. He orders the crowd to stand back, and punches some buttons on the remote. Seconds later the battle suit launches into the air.

Luthor's battle suit is faster than Superman has ever seen it before. Flames shoot from the heavy boots as the headless armor flies through the exit doors and up into the sky. A flood of people follow to see what will happen next.

Turn the page.

Outside, everyone stares up at the red sky. They watch in awe as the battle suit collides with one of the LexSphere drones, creating a huge explosion. Both Kryptonite-fueled gadgets are blown to bits in a fiery display. The red LexSphere light fades out and a shower of sparks falls to Earth.

Superman can feel the energy from the sun's rays restoring his strength. Then he hears Luthor's angry cries from the roof. The billionaire has lost two of his favorite machines.

Further away, but coming closer every second, Superman now hears two missiles speeding toward LEX-CON.

Turn to page 48.

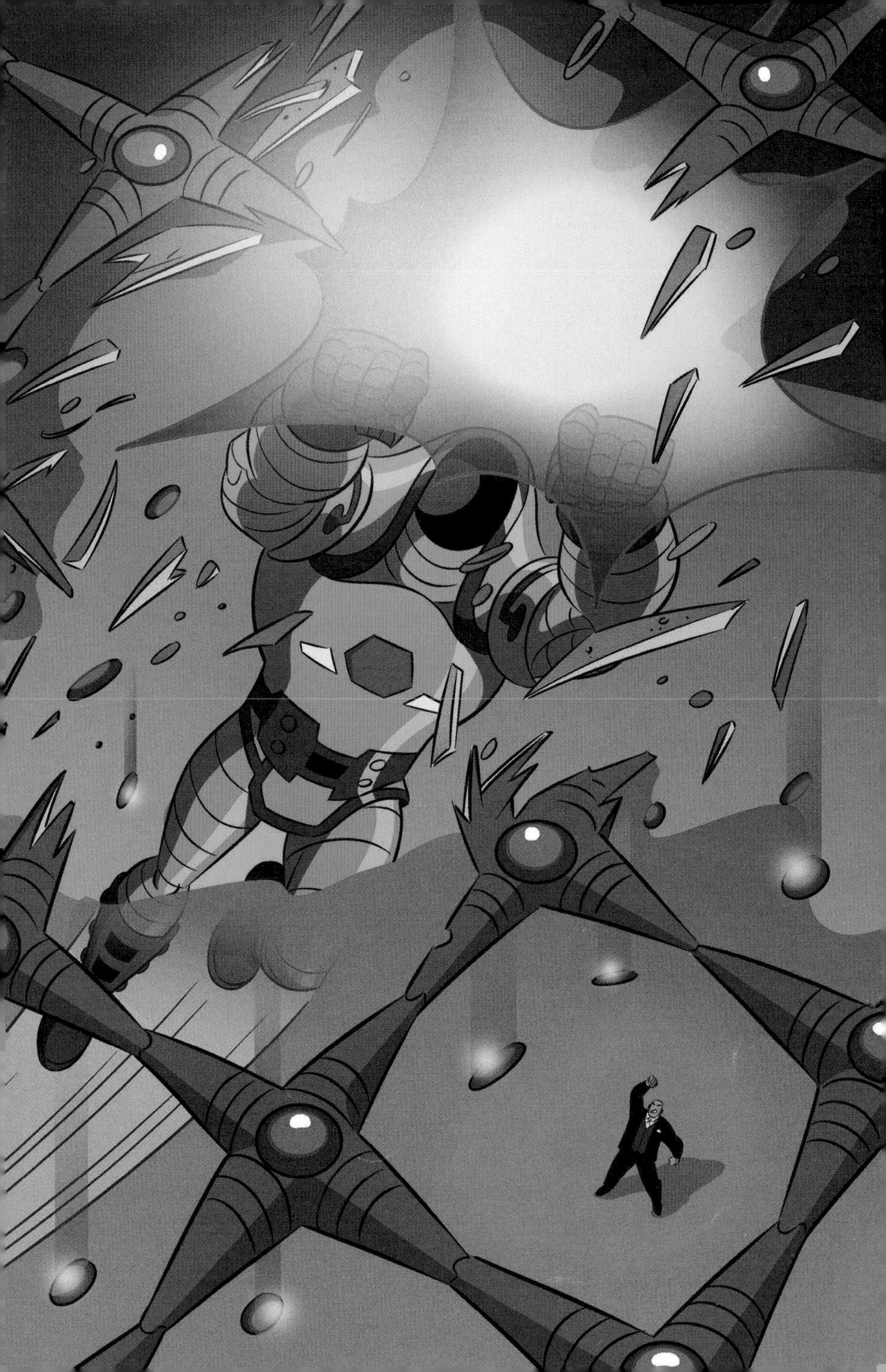

Feeling fully restored, Superman launches himself into the air. He flies at top speed toward the missiles and catches them as easily as footballs. Tucking one under each arm, he heads for the upper layers of the atmosphere. He hurls the weapons into outer space where they explode safely. Far, far below he can hear the cheers of the crowd at LEX-CON and the curses of the convention's creator. Superman smiles, but he doesn't rush back. He flies home slowly, enjoying his moment in the sun.

THE END

To follow another path, turn to page 11.

Everyone is staring at Luthor's battle suit and the super-charged villain about to engage in battle. Clark sees his chance and ducks behind the garbage dumpster. A moment later Superman swoops over the crowd — a blur of red and blue!

"What are *you* doing here?" Livewire sputters when she sees the hero. Sparks fall from her fingertips as her electrical charge fizzles.

"I thought Luthor might like to give his improved battle suit a real workout," Superman says, looking at the technician holding the remote.

The tech stands still — shocked by Superman's unexpected appearance. But while the tech did not expect Superman to show up, Lex Luthor had been waiting for him.

"I'll take that," Luthor says striding in and removing the remote from his employee's frozen hands. "I'd be happy to show you all of my suit's improvements, Superman!"

Turn the page.

"Hold on, Luthor," Livewire interrupts. "I thought we had a deal. You're paying me to fight your silly suit," she hisses.

"All right Sparky, how about we make a new deal," Luthor tells the electrified lady. "I'll still pay you. But now you and the suit fight Superman instead!"

Livewire looks from Luthor to the battle suit to Superman. She smiles widely and blue lightning crackles around her mouth and eyes. "I like the new deal," she growls. "You're on!"

Livewire spins in midair and directs a bolt of electricity at Superman. Superman is expecting it and dodges. Luthor, operating his battle suit from the ground, fires a green plasma blast. It catches Superman's left arm and sends the Man of Steel reeling.

Superman can't take on both Livewire and the battle suit at the same time. Just being near the suit is affecting his strength! He also doesn't want to fight with so many people nearby. Someone could get hurt.

Superman flies away from the convention center. As he flies by a large electronic billboard, he see the words on it change. Livewire is sending him a message. *Running away?* the sign reads. But Superman is not running away.

"Come and get me!" he shouts at the billboard.

Superman spots a large fountain nearby. He flies to it and blasts it with his icy breath. Then he touches down on the solid surface.

"You can't get away," Luthor yells, hovering down the street toward Superman. He is being carried by the battle suit.

The suit sets Luthor down and he uses the remote to move it toward Superman.

Superman feels the Kryptonite drain his strength. He also senses Livewire nearby.

"Got you now!" she shrieks, appearing beneath a set of nearby electrical wires.

Turn to page 58.

Clark leaves the man with his LexClean and goes back into the convention center. Although he detected a high-frequency radio signal, he could not decipher the message. He needs to find out where it was being sent.

Tuning in to his surroundings, Clark hears radio signals both higher and lower than humans can detect. But none of them are coming from the LexCleans. When he noticed the signal before it was right after the robot left the building.

I need to get another LexClean outside, he thinks.

Just then Jimmy Olsen comes rushing toward him. "Look what I got!" he exclaims excitedly. Following behind him is a brand new LexClean.

Thinking quickly, Clark says, "That's great Jimmy! You know, I think I dropped something outside. Would you mind helping me look for it?"

"Sure thing, Mr. Kent," Jimmy says.

Jimmy and his LexClean follow Clark out of the convention hall. When they step through the doors the LexClean sends out a radio signal, just like Clark hoped.

Jimmy can't hear it, but Superman does. A split second later he hears a tag, an indicator that a receiver has sensed the signal. The tag is coming from inside the building!

Clark spins around quickly and heads back inside the building.

"Where are you going?" Jimmy calls after him. "What are we even looking for?"

Clark doesn't stop to explain. He isn't sure what they're looking for, but he'll know when they find it. Heading across the floor of the convention, Clark sends Lois a text message: *Meet me behind the curtain on the LexClean stage.*

A few seconds later he gets a text back: *I'm already there.*

Turn the page.

The people around the LexClean stage are very excited about the robots. They don't even notice when Clark walks by and slips behind the curtain.

It's dark backstage, but using his infrared vision Clark has no problem making his way to Lois. He finds her beside a computer bank.

"Clark, check this out," she says. "This machine seems to be receiving information from the LexCleans."

Lois' discovery confirms Clark's suspicions. But then he detects something else. "You're right, Lois. And I think it may be sending instructions too."

"These robots aren't just for cleaning, are they?" Lois asks. She has a look on her face that Clark knows well. It's a look she gets when she knows she's got her story. "These things are spyware. They're gathering information and sending it back to Luthor's central computer."

Clark nods. "And if Luthor gets away with this he'll know everything about everyone in this city."

Turn to page 62.

In the red light beneath the dome Superman feels strange. There's more to the LexSphere than just blocking the sunrays that give Superman his power. It feels like his strength is actively being drained!

I have to break through that shield while I still have some strength, he thinks.

Gathering all his might he lifts off into the air with his fist aimed at the closest drone. As he gets closer Superman experiences the shield's draining effects more strongly. He feels weak, nauseous, and dizzy. But he forces himself upward. He tries to gain the speed needed to knock the drone out of formation with the others. He's not sure if he'll need to blast more than one. But he doesn't know if he has the strength to blast more than one anyway.

Turn the page.

Feeling his strength fading fast, Superman tries to fry the closest drone with his heat vision. He stares straight ahead while zooming upward. He has no problem getting the drone in his sights. But can't seem to focus his eyes well enough to blast it!

Shaking his head, he decides to rely on his one sure weapon — his fists. He'll have to stick with brute strength. Pushing down all feelings of weakness, Superman shuts his eyes and braces for impact.

CRACK!

His fist connects with the drone.

But the red Kryptonian light has weakened him too much. He doesn't have the power he needs. The impact sends him plummeting toward the ground.

Tumbling head over heels Superman lands with a terrible **CRASH!**

Luthor wastes no time getting on the microphone. "You see," he tells the crowd, "not even Superman can break through my shield."

Too weak to speak, Superman suddenly understands. The shield works for Luthor in two ways. It can keep Superman out . . . or trap him inside! But while the Kryptonian light works on him, there's no way to know if it can stop the missiles.

"No," Superman gasps weakly as the sound of the incoming missiles grows louder. The crowd looks up in the ghastly red light. In the distance two tiny silver objects are fast approaching.

Superman tries, but can't even summon the strength to stand.

Turn to page 65.

Superman looks down and blasts the ice with his heat vision. He zooms into the air at the same moment that Livewire's electric lightning hits the liquid water.

CRACK!

The noise is earsplitting and the charge backfires, shorting out Livewire's power. She falls to the concrete. Small wisps of smoke curl out of her blue hair.

"One down," Superman says to himself. Then he turns his attention to Luthor and his battle suit. "Two to go."

He spots Luthor punching buttons on the battle suit's controller. But the suit is nowhere to be seen.

"Why don't you get in it?" Superman shouts. It would be easier to take out the man and the machine at the same time.

Luthor laughs. "Oh no. This way is much more fun. I get to beat you and watch myself doing it!"

Superman's head throbs. The Kryptonite-laced suit must be close! He scans the sky overhead but his vision is blurry. He feels a piercing pain in the back of his head and sees a flash of green. He's blasted out of the sky and lands beside Luthor! His whole body goes limp, weighed down by a dull ache.

The battle suit hovers over the crumpled body of the Man of Steel as a crowd of onlookers gathers around.

"You see," Luthor laughs, gesturing to the crowd. "My suit can beat the strongest alien threat there is!"

Turn to page 61.

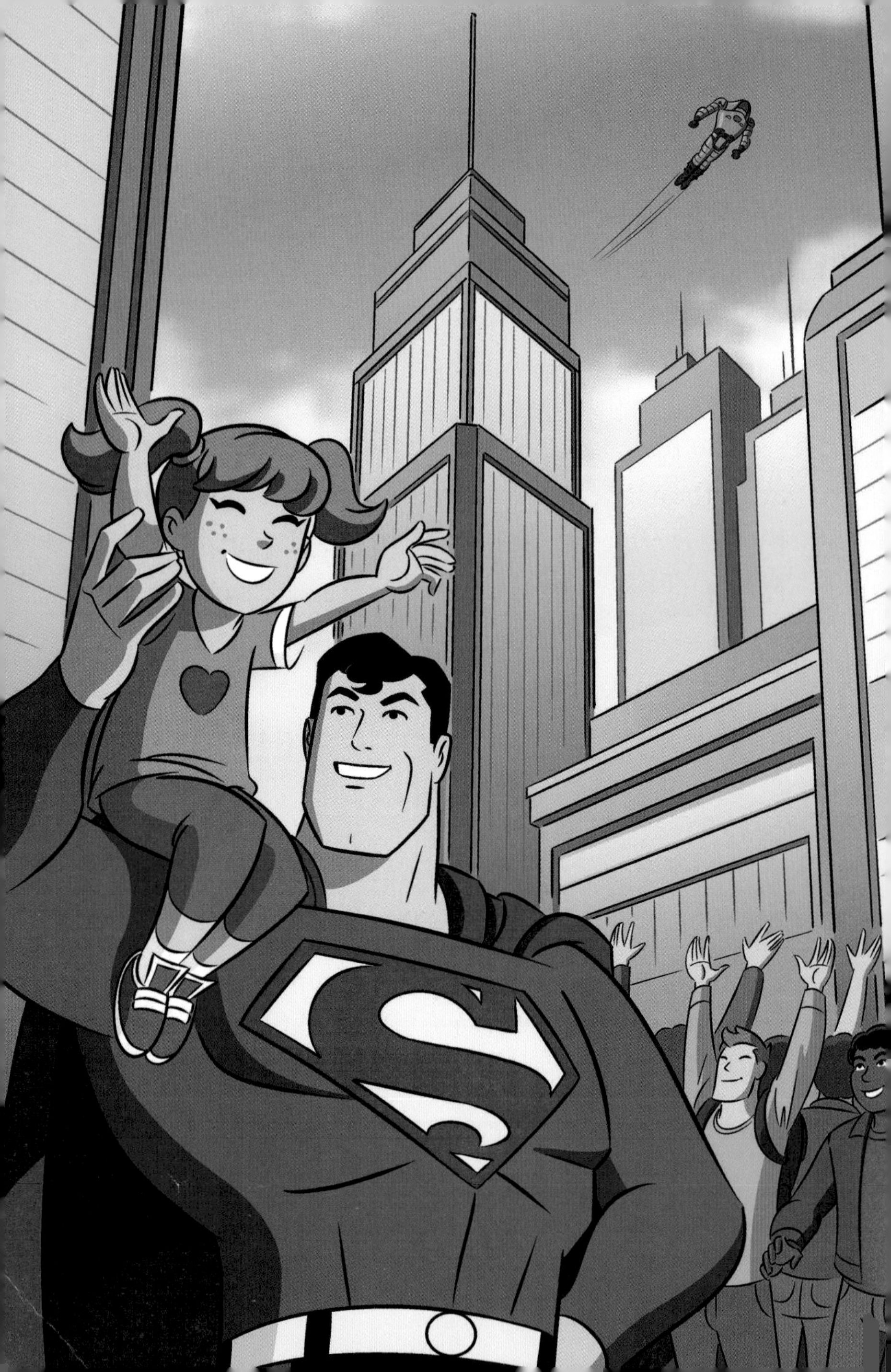

A young girl in the crowd steps up to Luthor. "But Superman's not a threat," she says. "He saves people. You're nothing but a rich bully!"

Superman draws strength from the girl's words, and from Earth's yellow sun. He feels his power returning.

The little girl is joined by others, all shouting at Luthor. The convention leader is so distracted by the crowd that he does not see Superman rise. The hero steps quietly up behind Luthor and takes the battle suit remote control from his hands. He quickly pushes some buttons and sends Luthor's battle suit hurtling toward space.

"No!" Luthor cries.

Superman smashes the remote in his fist. Then he lifts the little girl who stood up to Luthor onto his shoulder. "Power belongs in the hands of the merciful, Luthor," Superman says. "Maybe one day you'll learn that lesson yourself."

THE END

To follow another path, turn to page 11.

"Ah, you got me." Luthor steps around the curtain holding a flashlight. He shines it at Clark and Lois and walks slowly over to them. Behind him are three LexCleans. "I created these neat little robots to do my dirty work," he explains, chuckling. "With a LexClean in every house I would have all of the data I could ever need. I would be able to predict what people would need to buy before they knew themselves."

"It's called spying, Lex. And it's illegal," Lois says, standing to stare Luthor in the eye.

"Think of how helpful it could be," Luthor says, shrugging. "Like having on-the-scene reporters at every scene."

"Your home infiltration system is nothing like reporting," Lois says, offended.

"And your robotic spyware stops here," Clark adds.

"You're partly right, Kent. Something will stop here. But it isn't my LexCleans. It's your meddling!" Luthor growls.

Lex takes a step back and the three LexCleans behind him lurch forward with their arms outstretched. Lois ducks. Clark points to something behind Lex and shouts, "Look out!"

With Lex and Lois distracted, Clark reaches out and grabs a LexClean by the leg. He swings the robot in an arc on the floor, sweeping the other two robots off their feet. While Lex and Lois look stunned at the three downed robots, Clark quickly turns around. He removes his glasses and burns through the cords holding the heavy curtains.

When the curtains fall, Lex, his damaged LexCleans, and Lois stand blinking in the light. The crowd stares. Clark staggers forward rubbing his eyes. Then he grabs a microphone from a stunned technician.

Turn the page.

"Ladies and gentleman, on behalf of the *Daily Planet* we have an announcement," Clark says. Then he hands the mic to Lois and dials the police.

Lois glares at Luthor, who is too shocked at what's just happened to do anything. Then she turns and addresses the crowd.

"My colleague and I have discovered something that can't wait for tomorrow's front page," Lois says. "That's right, folks, Luthor's LexCleans aren't just for tidying up. They're for gathering dirt — on all of you! These robots are programmed to spy on you! We've informed the police, and they'll be seizing the LexCleans for further investigation."

"No!" Luthor finds his voice and protests loudly.

"I'm afraid so," Clark nods awkwardly. At that moment the police arrive and begin to gather up the LexCleans. There's nothing Luthor can do.

"Now that's the way to keep things clean," Lois says. Clark can't agree more.

THE END

To follow another path, turn to page 11.

Someone in the crowd screams as the silver objects draw closer to the convention center.

"Stop them!" someone else yells.

Luthor only laughs as panic spreads. "I couldn't stop them even if I wanted to," he says. "But don't worry. My LexSphere will protect us!"

Superman pulls his cape around himself. The special lining helps to protect him from the Kryptonite-powered light projected by the drones. He tries to think what to do, but his mind is fuzzy and unfocused. He feels weaker than ever. He hopes that Luthor is right about the LexSphere, and that it will protect the innocent people beneath it.

Turn the page.

KABOOM!

The first missile strikes the LexSphere high overhead with a deafening crash. People scream and try to take cover under anything they can find. The red light of the shield flickers and bits of hot metal rain down. But the LexSphere holds.

"Ha! Ha! Ha!" Luthor laughs into the mic, happy with the destruction. He acts like a child knocking over a block tower —

Then the second missile hits.

Superman rolls onto his back, sensing something awful is about to happen. The second missile does not explode on impact with the shield. The weakened LexSphere cannot hold. The missile breaks through the drones' bond and they fly apart in all directions. The red light of the dome goes out, and the missile continues on its path — straight toward the Metropolis convention center and the crowd below!

Superman leaps to his feet. He lacks the strength to fly. He closes his eyes and focuses on soaking in the yellow rays of the sun.

When Superman opens his eyes again, beams of light shoot out of them. Superman's powerful heat vision slices through the sky and connect with the missile speeding toward him.

KA-BLAM!

The second missile explodes into tiny sparks that burn out before they touch the ground.

There is a moment of stunned silence, and then the entire crowd erupts into loud cheers. Everyone except Lex Luthor.

Superman smiles at the bitter billionaire. "Sorry your shield didn't work, Luthor. But you're lucky I was here. Because of me, nobody got hurt."

Luthor scowls. "I'm not so sure I feel very lucky," he grumbles.

THE END

To follow another path, turn to page 11.

Superman charges out of the stairwell. Livewire and the battle suit hover over the crowd. The opponents circle each other. Every pair of eyes in the convention center is glued on them, waiting to see what will happen next.

When she spots Superman, Livewire's eyes light up with blue sparks of electricity. "Come to save the day, *Stooperman?*" she jeers.

The Innovention Tech controlling the battle suit looks happy to see Superman too. "Now I can show the world what this suit can really do!" he says excitedly.

The Man of Steel looks at the crowd of people below his enemies. They're too stunned to move.

Superman feels the effects of the Kryptonite lining of the battle suit. It's weakening his powers. He knows he can't take on the battle suit and Livewire at the same time. He needs to deal with the electric lady first.

"Can't have you getting all of the attention, can I?" Superman says, addressing Livewire. "Although I know you get a charge out of that."

The crowd laughs and Superman sees the anger in Livewire's eyes. Her attention is all on him, and she's mad, which is exactly what Superman wants.

Lifting into the air, but keeping his distance from the suit, Superman faces off with Livewire. "Do you want to show the people what you've got by battling an empty suit? Or by battling a living person?" Superman taunts her.

The crowd reacts with fear and excitement. It's more than Livewire can resist. She raises her hands and unleashes a brilliant blue electrical arc right at Superman.

The Man of Steel dodges and the bolt of lightning hits the cement wall of the building. Livewire tries to blast Superman again, but again Superman dodges her attack.

Turn to page 74.

Superman tears the panel off of the robot. Then he reaches into the cavity and silences the alarm. Once it's opened, the robot sends out another wireless signal and shuts down completely.

"Why would a cleaning robot have an alarm system?" Superman wonders out loud.

Lois looks puzzled too. "What's this?" She points at a red warning label on the LexClean's back. "Return to LexCorp for service," she reads. "Maybe that's how Luthor plans to make his money? By servicing the free machines for a price?"

"Maybe . . ." Superman says. But he isn't so sure. When he looks up he sees four more LexCleans coming toward them. "Maybe we can get some more information out of these guys," he suggests.

He walks toward the robots with his hands held up. "Sorry about your friend," he says. "I was just trying to get some information. Maybe one of you could help me out."

"No need to be alarmed," Superman says. He reaches for the back panel on one of the approaching LexCleans. He half-expects another alarm to sound, but does not expect what he finds. He yanks his hand back quickly when he touches something red-hot. The LexCleans have all activated heating elements on their back panels to keep them from being touched!

"524 must have been in communication with these other LexCleans," Superman tells Lois. "It warned them that it's back panel was tampered with. Now they've taken action to keep us out."

"But why would cleaning robots need to communicate with each other?" Lois asks.

"These robots are definitely designed for more than just cleaning," Superman says. "I'm sure they're communicating with more than just one another. I suspect they're gathering data and sending it to a database."

"For LexCorp," Lois finishes for him. "These robots are nothing but *spyware*!"

Turn to page 77.

Clark darts under a stairwell and emerges dressed as Superman. Luthor spots him immediately and cackles with glee. "Just the guy I've been waiting for!" he says into his microphone. "How do you like my LexSphere, Superman?" he asks with a smile.

"I don't," Superman says.

"Oh, but I made it just for you!" Luthor says, pretending to pout. Then his expression changes, and a wicked smile creeps across his face. "Well, that's not quite true . . . I made it so that we won't need you. I made it to protect us from aliens like you!"

The crowd parts so Superman can approach. He walks slowly toward Luthor. He doesn't want Lex to see that his power is fading in the red light. "But who will protect us from *you*, Lex?" he asks. "What if your LexSphere doesn't hold? Isn't it a bit reckless to risk the lives of all of these people with your little test?"

"The people are protected," Lex laughs. "You're the only one in jeopardy!"

"Look!" Someone in the crowd points up at two silver objects, like tiny stars over the red dome. The missiles are coming closer!

Several people scream. More rush for the stairs. But they're all trapped inside the dome.

Superman knows it's now or never. He gathers his remaining strength and flies up toward the drones with a single fist extended.

"Stop him!" Luthor shouts to his technicians. "He's trying to break the shield!"

Superman ignores everything that's happening below. His energy is leaving him. He feels weak, sick, and slightly dizzy. He focuses on a single drone. He just has to hit it with enough force to knock it out of formation.

Turn to page 81.

Suddenly a voice pipes up from below. "I thought Luthor was sending a worthy opponent to show off the battle suit," the tech with the remote sneers. "I can dispatch both of you with one blow!"

"Just try it, geek!" Livewire snaps back.

Superman sees the armored hand of the battle suit glowing green, preparing a Kryptonite blast. Livewire sees it too. Lightning shoots from her fingertips. It hits the suit, but the armor is unaffected. The armor continues to charge.

Superman knows that in his weakened state the Kryptonite blast will be too much. He needs a shield. The only thing that can shield him from Kryptonite is lead — just like in the leaded glass case that was holding the suit!

With lightning speed, Superman flies into the case and seals himself inside. The Kryptonite plasma discharges from the battle suit's gun arm. It blasts Livewire back into the tank of submersible drones, where her power is shorted out completely. But Superman remains unaffected inside the glass display case.

"One down, one to go!" The tech pushes buttons on the remote to open the case, but it's already too late. Superman has frozen the workings from inside with a blast of his super breath. Nothing moves. Inside the leaded glass Superman is protected. "Come out and fight!" the frustrated tech yells.

"Yes, Superman," Lex Luthor steps out of the crowd and circles the glass case, sizing up the Man of Steel. "Come out and fight."

Superman keeps his eyes on Luthor. While he may be safe in the case, he is also trapped.

Taking the remote from his tech, Luthor begins pushing buttons. The battle suit turns to fly at the case with its fists out. "There's more than one way to crack a case," Luthor says as the battle suit hovers over Superman's head. "If you won't come out, we'll come in."

Then Luthor pushes the button.

Turn the page.

The battle suit speeds toward the case. The crowd flees — certain that an explosion is coming. Then at the last second, Superman zaps the frozen door with his heat vision to melt away the ice. It opens and he zooms out of the case to dodge the battle suit.

"No!" Luthor pushes buttons frantically but can't turn his battle suit around in time. It flies straight into the case. Superman quickly pushes the door closed and freezes it in place once again.

Luthor stomps his feet and turns red in the face. "Curse you, Superman!" he shouts.

"Just helping you put away your toys, Lex," Superman replies calmly. He wags his finger at the angry billionaire. "At least until you can learn to play nicely."

THE END

To follow another path, turn to page 11.

"That's right," Superman agrees. "With a LexClean in every home, Luthor would know everything about everyone. He would know what people wanted to buy almost before they did. He would know people's habits, their movements —"

Superman stops and watches as several more LexCleans approach. Soon they're surrounded.

"And if he's able to command them from a central computer . . ." Lois adds, trailing off.

"He could have an instant army right here in the city!" Superman says. He looks around slowly at the LexCleans surrounding him. "That is, if they're trained for combat."

Superman whirls and hits the closest LexClean with a powerful punch. His fist dents the metal and sends the robot flying into the one behind it. Two LexCleans are down. But within seconds the other LexCleans circling them advance on the Man of Steel. All around the convention hall the rest of the LexCleans are alerted and begin moving toward Superman and Lois.

Turn the page.

Luckily the LexCleans are no match for Superman. He easily takes out ten of them with his fists. But the robots continue to communicate with each other, and begin to use new defenses. When Superman punches the eleventh robot, the super hero gets a powerful electrical shock. It's so strong that it knocks him backward.

"Don't touch them," he warns the rest of the people in the convention center. "They're electrified!"

Superman has to try a new tactic. Drawing a deep breath, he blows a powerful icy blast, flash-freezing six LexCleans at once. He turns to blast another group. But they're ready for Superman's next attack. Their bodies are hot, just like their back panels. So Superman's icy breath has no effect on them.

The LexCleans communicate and adjust quickly. It's as if they're one giant organism adapting continuously.

Turn to page 80.

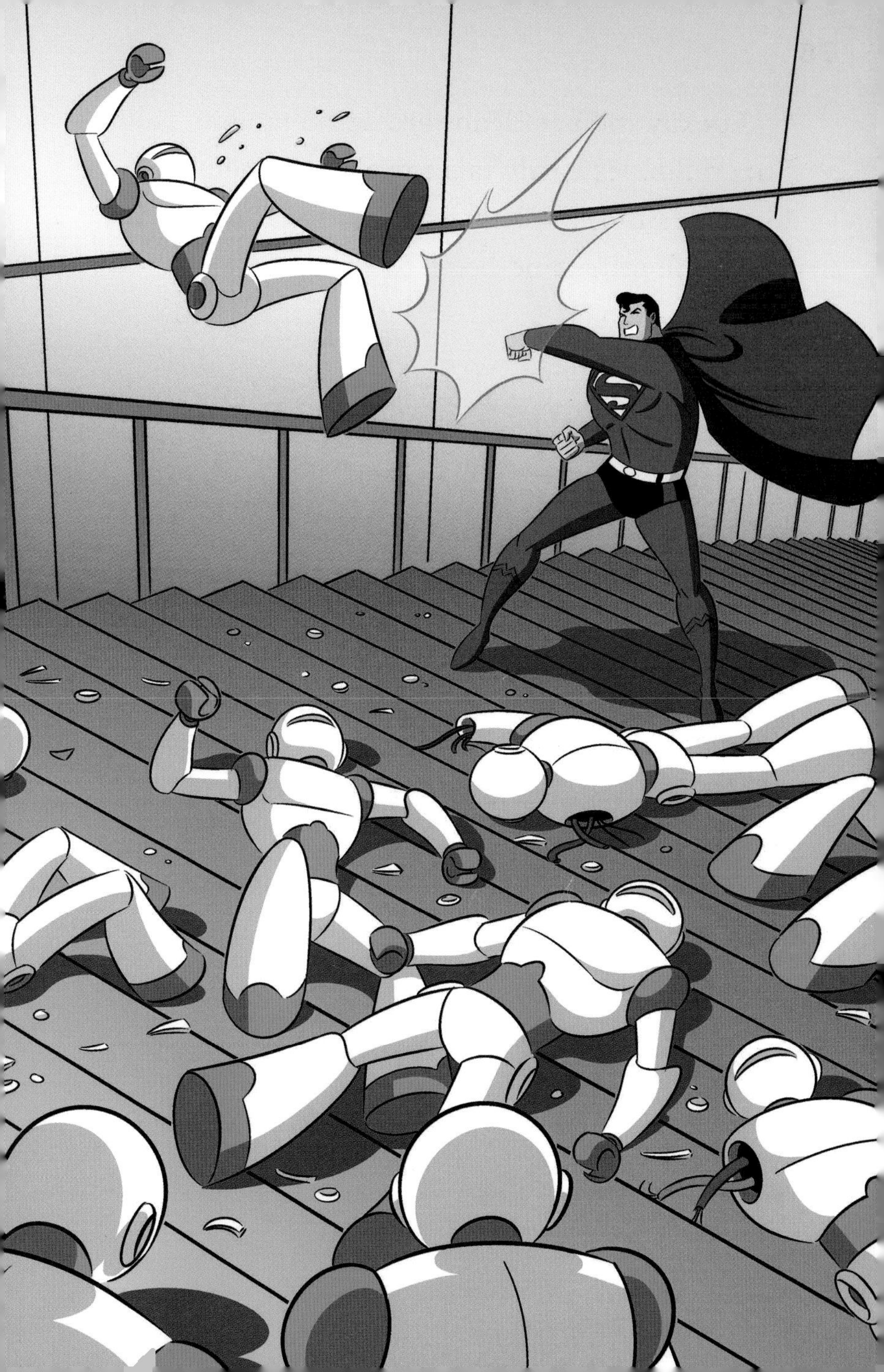

Superman focuses on the high-frequency radio signals the LexCleans use to communicate. He detects a tag — a signal indicating that a message has been received. It's coming from the stage.

Superman heads for the curtains. The LexCleans swarm all over the Man of Steel, trying to burn and shock him. Suddenly, Superman flings the robots in all directions. Using a downed LexClean, Superman sweeps a path to the stage where he finds the LexCleans' central computer.

"Luthor's command station," Superman says. He easily disables the control station with his heat vision. The LexCleans stop in their tracks. They're useless without their shared computer brain.

"What have you done?" Luthor asks, storming in from outside.

"Just a little demonstration of my own," Superman says. He turns to Lois who is taking notes rapidly. Meanwhile, Jimmy is snapping pictures of the scene. "But don't worry, Lex. I think you'll still get your headline!"

THE END

To follow another path, turn to page 11.

As he closes in on one of the drones, Superman is nearly overcome. The draining red light is sapping not only his powers, but also his life force! He tears his eyes away from the target for one moment to look at the hundreds of innocent people on the ground. He cannot fail them.

The people are screaming and pointing, but not just at Superman. There's something else in the sky with him. One of Luthor's technicians has launched Luthor's battle suit to try to knock Superman out of the sky!

The battle suit quickly closes in on the Man of Steel. Superman can feel it growing closer. He can feel his powers weakening faster from the combined red and green Kryptonite. He begins to lose speed.

At last he reaches his target.

BOOM!

He rams into the drone fist first. The pain he feels is unfamiliar. The blow steals away every bit of his remaining strength. Superman begins to fall back toward the convention center far below.

Turn the page.

But as he falls, above him the drone he hit wobbles — and blinks out.

All it takes is one broken link in the chain. Within seconds, the rest of the drones stop beaming their red light, and the glowing LexSphere disappears.

Nothing stands between Metropolis and Lex Luthor's test missiles.

But as soon as the dome fails, the sun's yellow rays hit Superman. He feels his powers quickly returning. He stops hurting, but he still doesn't have the strength to fly! There is still more Kryptonite weakening him.

The mystery is solved when Luthor's Kryptonite-powered battle suit zooms into view. Luthor is operating it from the ground, and trying to take Superman out! With his last remaining strength, Superman grabs onto the flying armor. It makes him sick to be so close to the suit, but he has to find a way to stop the missiles from striking the convention center.

Using his head, Superman bashes the camera attached to the battle suit that Luthor is using to navigate. Without a camera view Luthor is flying blind!

The battle suit's rocket-arm begins to glow green. It's preparing to discharge a Kryptonite plasma blast. Superman ignores the pain in his head and aims the arm at the missiles. The green plasma blast hits both missiles, blowing them out of the air.

With the people safe below, Superman lets go of the suit and begins to fall. He closes his eyes and soaks up the sun's rays as he plummets. The solar energy recharges him enough so that he can slow his descent. He lands on the convention center roof to cheers and applause. But the thing that truly makes the Man of Steel smile is Lex Luthor's enormous frown.

THE END

To follow another path, turn to page 11.

Superman steps out from behind the stairway door. At the same moment, Livewire emerges from a nearby power outlet. She hovers over the crowd. Superman flies up beside her. He does his best to ignore the sickening effects of the Kryptonite in the battle suit.

"Ha!" the technician chuckles gleefully below. "Looks like I have two foes! Now I can truly demonstrate the punishing power of Lex Luthor's battle suit!"

The crowd is stunned. They didn't expect a mock battle — and certainly didn't expect Superman!

Livewire isn't happy about it. "Leave it to you to steal the show. You'll do anything to feed your ego," she snaps at Superman. Angry sparks drip from her fingertips. But she doesn't have much time to complain. Luthor's battle suit zooms in unexpectedly and crashes into Livewire in midair. She hurtles backward, hitting the far wall with a sickening thud. The lights in the convention center flicker.

Turn to page 86.

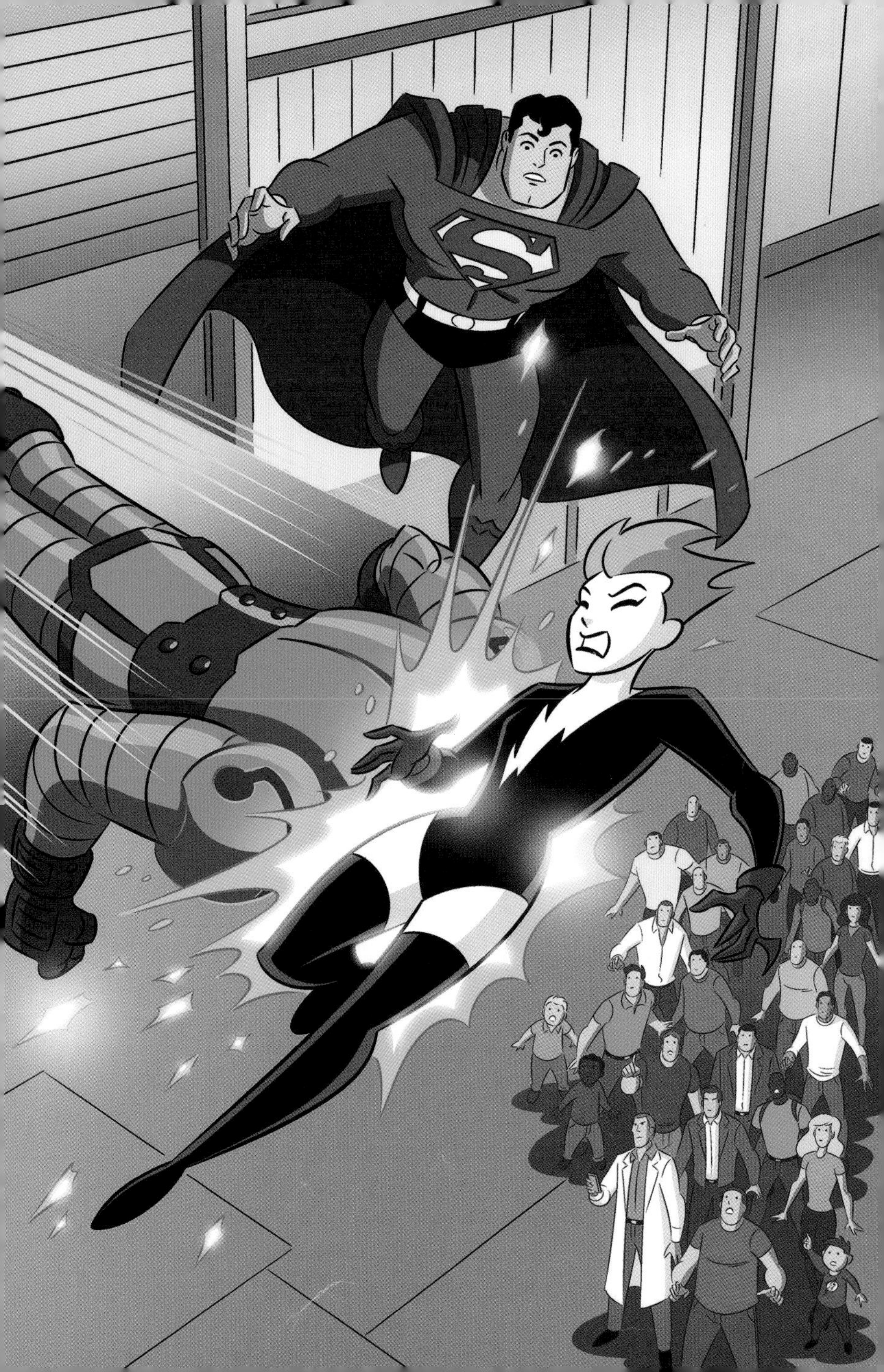

But the blue-haired baddie recovers quickly. "Is that all you've got?" she taunts the tech controlling the suit. "Brute force?" her eyes glimmer.

Superman watches as Livewire unleashes a super-charged lightning storm at the battle suit. Blue electricity arcs all over the purple and green armor. But when it stops, the suit is undamaged. One of its huge arms begins to glow green — readying an attack of its own.

Before the battle suit discharges its plasma bolt, Superman advances. With super speed and strength he flies at the battle suit and delivers a punishing blow. The suit is thrown halfway across the convention center. Superman prepares to strike again, but is hit from behind by one of Livewire's shocking attacks. The electrical jolt adds to the weakening effects of the Kryptonite in the battle suit. Superman is temporarily stunned.

"Don't attack me, hit the battle suit," Superman gasps.

Livewire cackles. "But I've never seen you like this, Superman," the ex DJ says. "You're so . . . *weak*. It's pathetic." She holds her hands out to hit Superman with another electrical blast. But she doesn't see the battle suit approaching behind her.

The suit smashes Livewire out of the air. She is thrown into the tank of submersible drones below. The water short-circuits the villain and causes a blackout through the entire building. LEX-CON goes dark.

But Superman can see in darkness. He sees the technician pushing buttons on his glowing screen, readying the battle suit for another attack.

Superman senses that the armor is targeting him. It follows him as he flies toward the exit. He punches through the doors and zooms up to the roof, where Luthor is getting ready to demonstrate his LexSphere.

Turn to page 95.

VRONK! VRONK! VRONK!

Superman backs away from the LexClean blasting its noisy alarm.

"What's with the alarm?" Lois asks Superman with her hands over her ears. "Does Luthor think people are going to steal his robots? Why would they, if everyone has one?"

"Luthor's hiding something," Superman says as a tech worker comes over and deactivates the alarm. "He doesn't want anyone outside LexCorp tinkering with his LexCleans."

"Could that be how he plans to make a profit on these things?" Lois asks. "There could be some money in being the only company that can repair them."

"Not enough," Superman shakes his head. He spots another LexClean following its new owner and walks toward it. The LexClean turns and sounds its alarm before Superman even reaches out a hand!

VRONK! VRONK! VRONK!

Lois laughs and covers her ears again. "They're onto you, Superman!"

An annoyed tech worker rushes over to deactivate the second alarm.

"I didn't touch this one," Superman says holding his hands up and backing away. Then he turns to Lois. "I really didn't touch it. The first robot must have signaled the others that I was some sort of threat."

"So the robots talk to each other?" Lois asks.

Superman nods. "Yes, they must share information with each other . . . and probably with someone else."

Superman closes his eyes and listens more closely to the high-frequency radio signals of the LexCleans. Finally he hears the faint sound of a receiver tagging the incoming information. It's coming from the lower level.

"Lois, I think I may have found your story," Superman says. He motions for the reporter to follow and heads for the stairs.

Turn the page.

The convention floor is crowded and growing more crowded all the time. People are rushing to get their very own LexCleans. Superman zigs in and out of the people with Lois on his heels. They pass several robots, and Superman hears each one sending a signal. He only wishes he knew what they're sending!

Finally they reach the door to the stairs and start down. Before they reach the landing they hear the door open behind them.

"LexCleans are following us!" Lois yells, but Superman already knows.

Three LexCleans pursue them down the stairs. These robots aren't looking to clean up any messes. They want to stop Superman.

"Lois, stand back!" Superman instructs. He turns and hits the robots with his icy breath, freezing them. The ice-covered LexCleans topple down the stairs, unable to move. But in an instant six more LexCleans storm through the door.

Turn to page 98.

Clark staggers toward the elevators. When the doors close, he quickly covers the security camera and changes. When the elevator doors open again, Superman emerges!

Even inside the convention center, Superman feels weakened by the draining red light of the LexSphere.

One of Luthor's technicians is demonstrating the battle suit, flying it over a small crowd.

"May I try?" Superman asks. The tech is so startled to see the Man of Steel that he hands over the remote without question. Superman quickly studies the controls. Even though his head is pounding from the LexSphere and the Kryptonite-powered battle suit, he is swiftly able to understand the device.

He punches in a location, sending the battle suit out the door and up to the roof. Superman can't fly after it, so he takes the elevator.

A moment later Superman and the battle suit both appear on the roof.

Turn the page.

The billionaire is excited to see the Man of Steel. "Superman!" Luthor exclaims. "And my battle suit! What a delightful surprise."

"Luthor you have to stop those missiles," Superman says, keeping the suit's remote hidden in his cape. "You are putting people in danger."

Luthor only laughs. "That's what the LexSphere is for!" he says. "Besides, I don't want to waste this marvelous opportunity to battle you on equal footing — at last!"

Luthor steps off of his podium and walks to the battle suit. He pushes a button to open the suit and climbs inside. The specially designed armor closes around him. "Now we can finally show the world that my technology is more than enough to defeat your alien powers!" Using the controls inside the suit Luthor lifts into the air.

"Come now, Superman. Don't be shy," he calls out.

Turn to page 94.

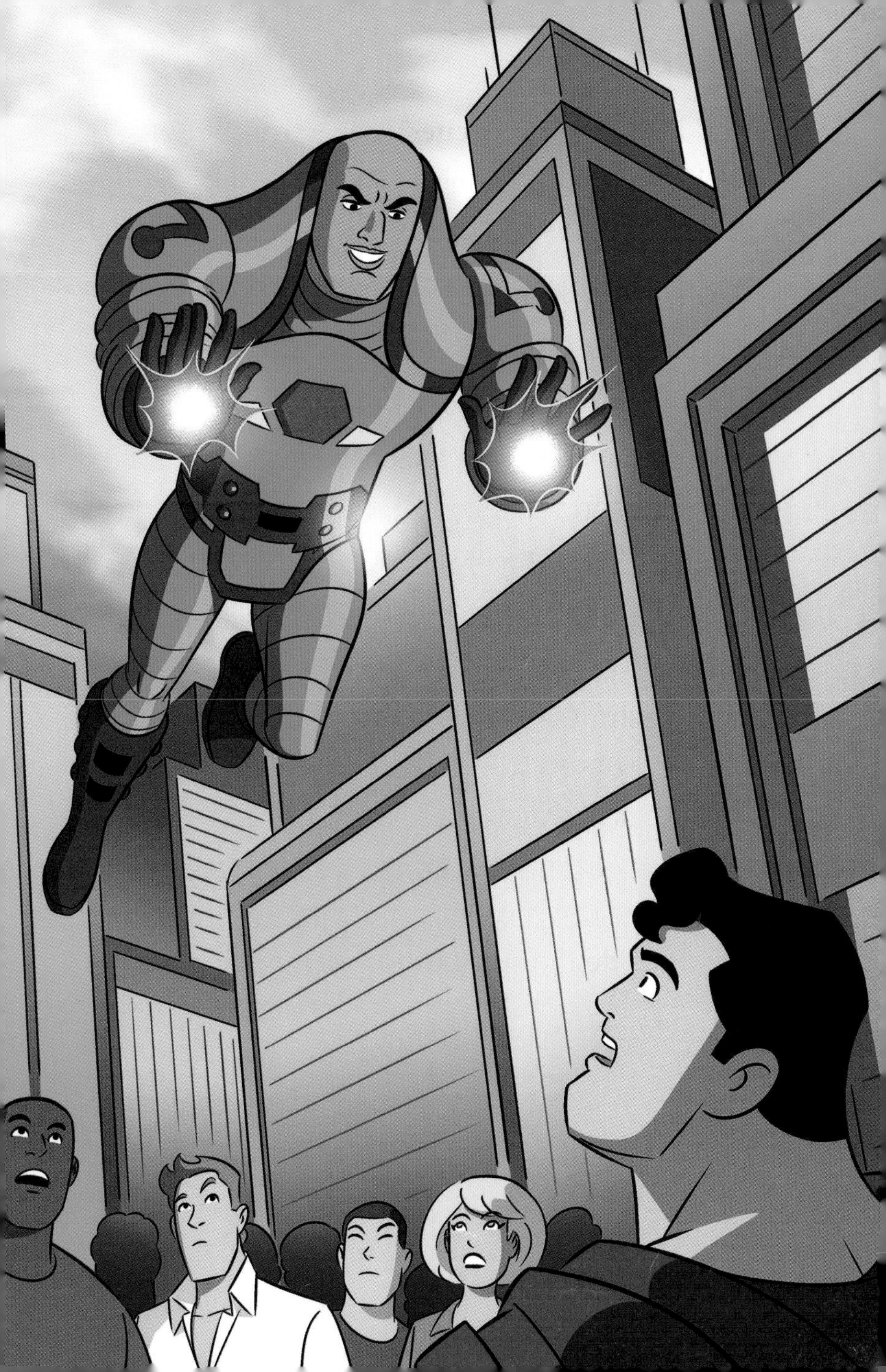

Superman stays on the ground. "This is your last warning, Luthor. You need to stop those missiles," he shouts.

"Or what?" Luthor asks. He aims his energy blaster at Superman and fires.

Superman is blasted back by a blinding green plasma bolt.

"Come on, Superman!" Luthor yells angrily. "I've been waiting for this. Aren't you going to fight me? Or maybe you can't. Has my LexSphere already turned you into Not-So-Superman?" Luthor laughs at his own joke while Superman struggles to his feet.

The Man of Steel tries to hide how much Luthor's blast took out of him. He hopes he has enough strength left to carry out his plan.

"You want to knock something out, Luthor?" Superman asks. "How about this?"

Turn to page 102.

"Well look who's here!" Lex Luthor says to the crowd on the roof. "Superman! And my battle suit!" The billionaire bad guy speaks in a hushed tone into a wireless radio. He tells the tech controlling the battle suit to stand down. "I'll take it from here," he whispers.

The battle suit stops charging after Superman and hovers beside Luthor like some sort of attack dog.

"You're just in time, Superman. I was about to show everyone my LexSphere. It's a light shield capable of protecting people from alien threats . . . like you," Luthor says with a smile.

Superman narrows his eyes. His head still pounds. The Kryptonite in the suit is taking a toll. He needs to contain it . . . somehow.

"All I have to do is push this button and my drones will do the rest." Luthor holds up another remote control device and activates the shield.

Turn the page.

The drones launch into the air and spread out over the crowd while Luthor chuckles to himself. "I think you're going to like this Superman. You see, this shield can contain anything. And while it keeps me and other Earthlings safe, it will keep you from getting the power you need to dominate us!"

Superman can barely believe his ears. His head already feels like it's about to split open. He can't allow Luthor to block out the solar energy that gives him his powers.

"No!" he roars and launches himself at Lex Luthor. He tackles the billionaire and sends the remote flying out of his hands.

The extra effort saps Superman's energy, and he struggles to get back to his feet. But Luthor leaps to his feet easily. He runs to the battle suit and scrambles inside.

"I'm afraid your time is out, Superman!" Luthor flies up using the jets on the battle suit. He hovers over Superman as he lies helpless on the roof.

It looks like the game is over. But Luthor has overlooked one thing.

"Superman!" Lois Lane picks up the LexSphere remote and tosses it to the downed hero.

Superman catches it and begins punching its buttons. Within seconds the LexSphere drones fly closer to Luthor and the battle suit.

Luthor laughs sarcastically, not understanding what Superman is up to. "I'd fire on you, but I don't want to damage my LexSphere controller!" Luthor jeers.

Soon the drones swarm around Lex and Superman pushes one last button. Red lights beam from the angled sides of each drone. They connect to form a shield all around Luthor — trapping him and his dangerous armor.

"You'd fire on me, Lex. But you can't!" Superman laughs back. "Looks to me like you're caught in your own trap!"

THE END

To follow another path, turn to page 11.

Superman draws a deep breath and unleashes another freezing blast at the new LexCleans coming down the stairs. But instead of freezing them, they instantly shrug off the icy blast. These robots have super-heated their bodies. The LexCleans Superman froze moments before have warned the others. Superman has to try something new.

"Keep going!" he calls to Lois. "You look for the radio receiver while I hold them off. And find something to hold onto!" Superman cautions her before filling his lungs.

Superman unleashes a mighty blast of air at the oncoming robots. He blows with such strength that the stairwell is filled with hurricane force winds. The LexCleans are blown about wildly. They smash into the walls and fall clattering down the metal stairs.

Below he can hear Lois. She escaped the storm and has reached the lower level.

Turn to page 100.

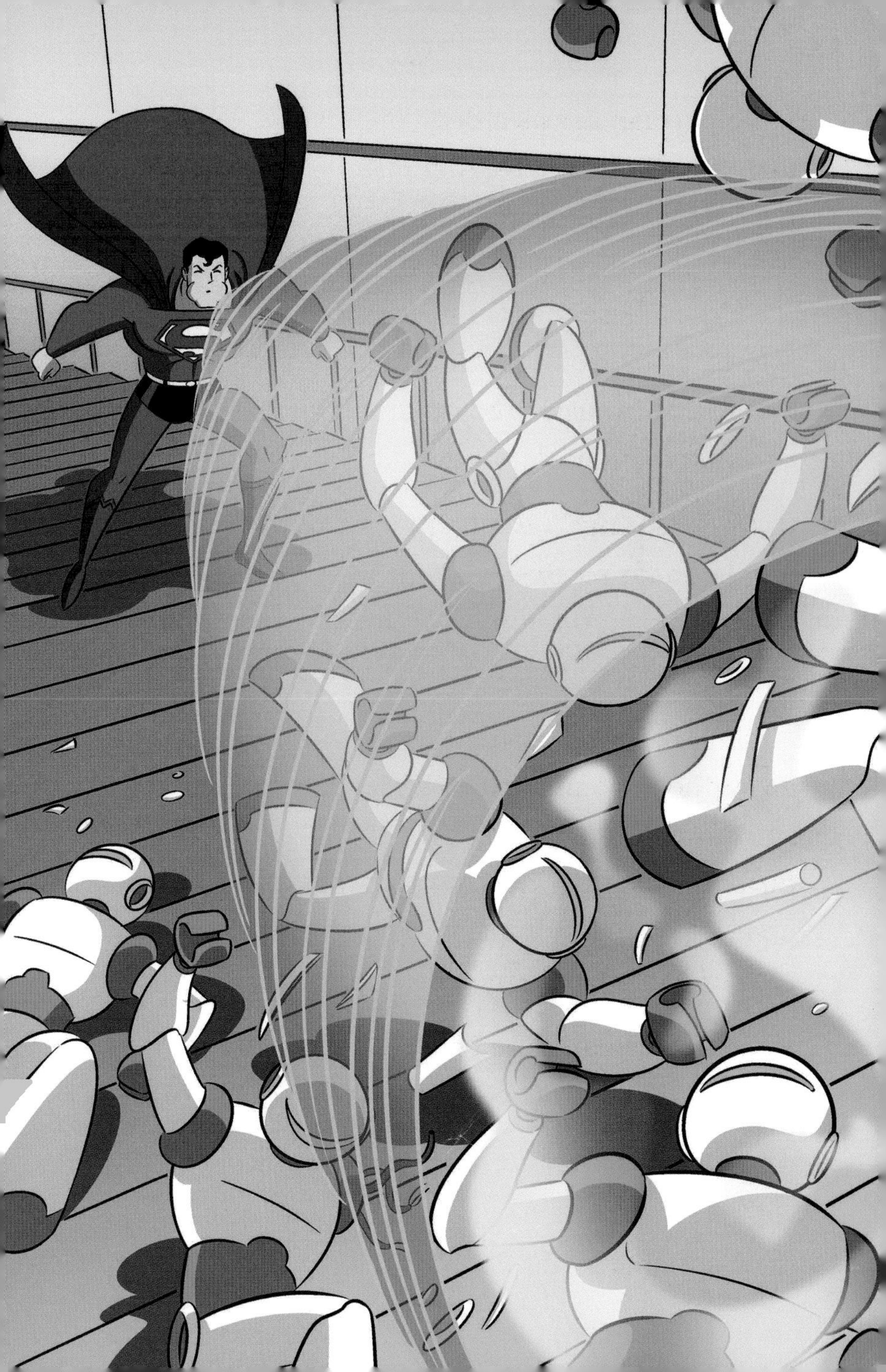

But the robots' attack isn't over. The door at the top of the stairs opens again, and twelve new LexCleans descend on Superman.

I'm sure they've adapted somehow, the Man of Steel thinks to himself, *but how?* Superman creates a new windstorm in the stairwell. The LexCleans lean into the gale, but remain on their feet. They're using electromagnets to attach themselves to the metal stairs!

Luckily Superman isn't out of options yet — he can always rely on his super-strength! He rushes up the stairs and takes the first LexClean out with a crippling punch. Though the robots are red-hot, Superman is moving too fast to be burned. He punches the next LexClean so hard it takes out several behind it. As the rear robots stumble, Superman picks them off easily.

But soon the door opens again.

Staring down an army of thirty LexCleans, Superman prepares for another round of fighting. The robots start to advance, but then come to a sudden halt! Their heads hang slack and their internal lights go dark.

They've been deactivated!

Superman races down the stairs to find Lois beside a large central computer. She's studying the screen, and snapping pictures with her phone.

"Nice work," he says. "You shut them all down."

"And that's not all I'm going to shut down," Lois says. "Look at this! The LexCleans aren't cleaning robots, they're spyware. They're designed to send information from people's homes directly to LexCorp."

"And with a fleet of robots blanketing the city, and under his control . . . Lex would have an instant mechanized army," Superman adds.

Lois looks at the robots littering the floor. "So much for LexCleans," she says shaking her head. "This is just one more big Lex mess."

THE END

To follow another path, turn to page 11.

Superman pulls out the controller for Luthor's battle suit and quickly overrides the manual controls. Luthor frantically pushes buttons in the suit, but nothing happens.

"For our next demonstration, we're going to see which is stronger, the battle suit or your LexSphere!" Superman shouts.

"Nooo!" Luther lets out a frustrated yell, but it's no use.

Superman has control. He locks in a flight path and sets the suit's jets to maximum speed. Luthor and the battle suit take off like a rocket, growing smaller in the sky until they connect with one of the LexSphere drones.

The small drone is blasted out of formation. The red light it had been projecting blinks out. Once it does, the rest of the drones go out too. The eerie red light is completely extinguished, allowing yellow sunlight to flood the convention center roof.

Superman drops to his knees and let's the sun's rays recharge him. He feels his strength returning. But he also hears something that strikes a chill into his heart. The approaching missiles are coming in fast!

Getting to his feet, Superman raises his fist into the air and takes off. His body is still sluggish, but the longer he is in sunlight the stronger he feels. He races toward the two missiles hoping his strength will be restored enough. He's not sure he'll be able to take the explosive impact of both missiles, or even one. But he suddenly knows what he must do.

Superman intercepts the first missile. Wrapping his arms around it, Superman uses his strength to change its direction, aiming it up and away from the planet. Then he lets go. The missile continues on its new path out of Earth's atmosphere.

Turn the page.

Then Superman targets the second missile, which is closing in fast on Metropolis. On the convention center roof, the crowd begins to point and scream. The missile is so close they can see it! It's coming right for them! But they watch amazed as Superman catches it, and then pulls it up and away. When it's clear that they're safe they begin to cheer wildly.

Superman pauses, watching the second missile head into space. He hears the distant booms when they explode. Satisfied, he starts to fly home, but pauses once more and pulls out the battle suit's remote control. He left Luthor flying off into space, but he has a plan for the reckless billionaire. He punches in a new destination. A special delivery is about to land at the Metropolis Police Department.

THE END

To follow another path, turn to page 11.

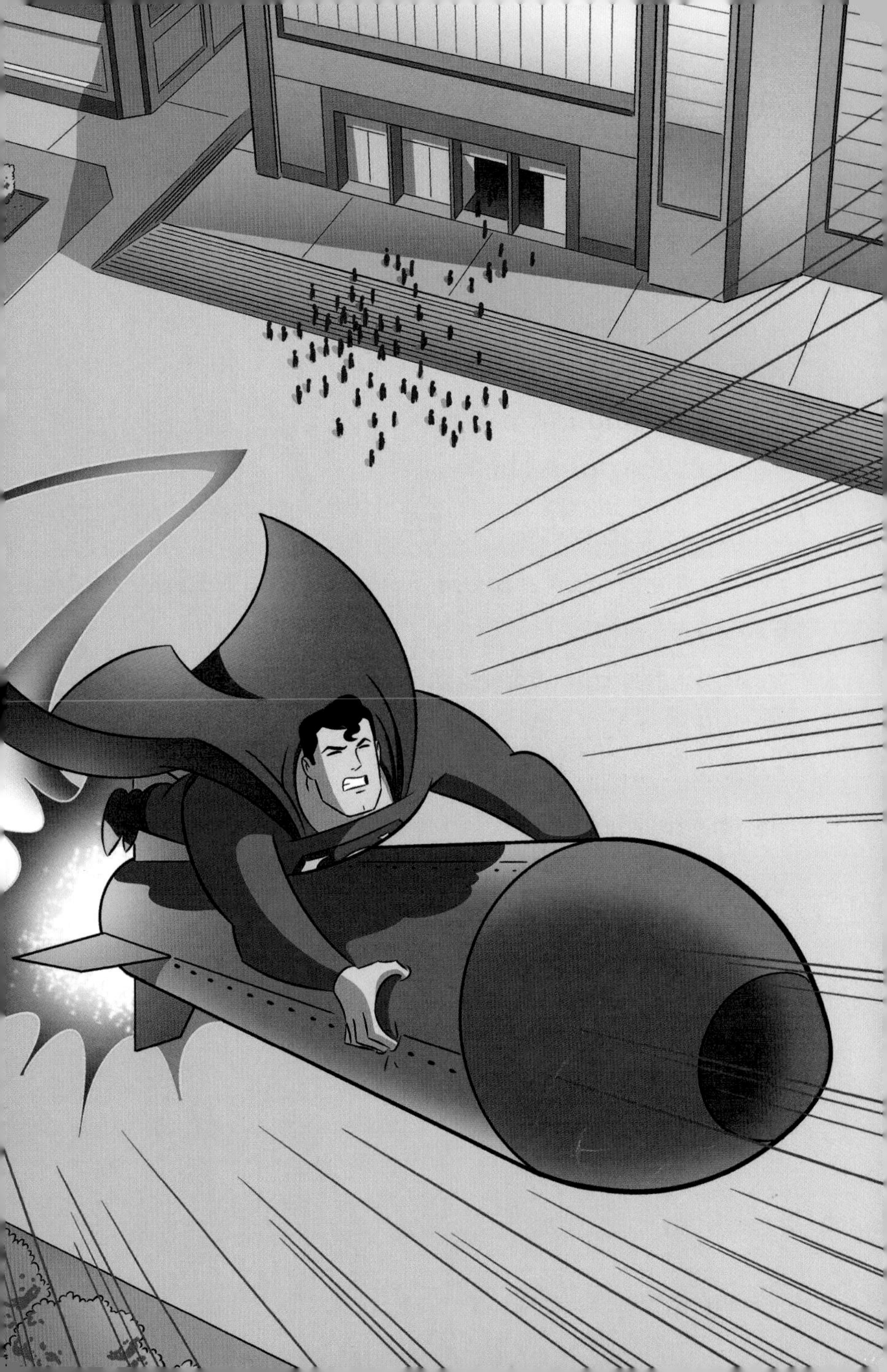

AUTHOR

Sarah Hines Stephens has authored more than 60 books for children, and written about all kinds of characters, from Jedi to princesses. Though she has some stellar red boots, she is still holding out for an invisible plane and thinks a Lasso of Truth could come in handy parenting her two wonder kids. When she is not writing, gardening, or saving the world by teaching about recycling, Sarah enjoys spending time with her heroic husband and super friends.

ILLUSTRATOR

Darío Brizuela was born in Buenos Aires, Argentina, in 1977. He enjoys doing illustration work and character design for several companies, including DC Comics, Marvel Comics, Image Comics, IDW Publishing, Titan Publishing, Hasbro, Capstone Publishers, and Disney Publishing Worldwide. Darío's work can be found in a wide range of properties, including *Star Wars Tales*, *Ben 10*, *DC Super Friends*, *Justice League Unlimited*, *Batman: The Brave & The Bold*, *Transformers*, *Teenage Mutant Ninja Turtles*, *Batman 66*, *Wonder Woman 77*, *Teen Titans Go!*, *Scooby Doo! Team Up*, and *DC Super Hero Girls*.

GLOSSARY

database (DAY-tuh-bays)—a collection of organized information on a computer

decipher (dih-SY-fuhr)—to make out the meaning of something

electromagnet (i-lek-troh-MAG-nuht)—a temporary magnet created when an electric current flows through a conductor

frequency (FREE-kwuhn-see)—the number of sound waves that pass a location in a certain amount of time

infrared (in-fruh-RED)—light waves in the electromagnetic spectrum between visible light and microwaves

lure (LOOR)—to attract or draw something closer

nauseous (NAW-shuhss)—to feel sick to one's stomach

plasma (PLAZ-muh)—a highly charged state of matter

receiver (ri-SEE-vur)—a device that receives radio signals and turns them into sound or pictures

savvy (SAV-ee)—knowledgeable, shrewd, and cunning

submersible (suhb-MURS-uh-buhl)—a small underwater craft powered by motors

transmitter (transs-MIT-uhr)—a device that converts sound waves and sends them out as radio or TV signals

LEX LUTHOR

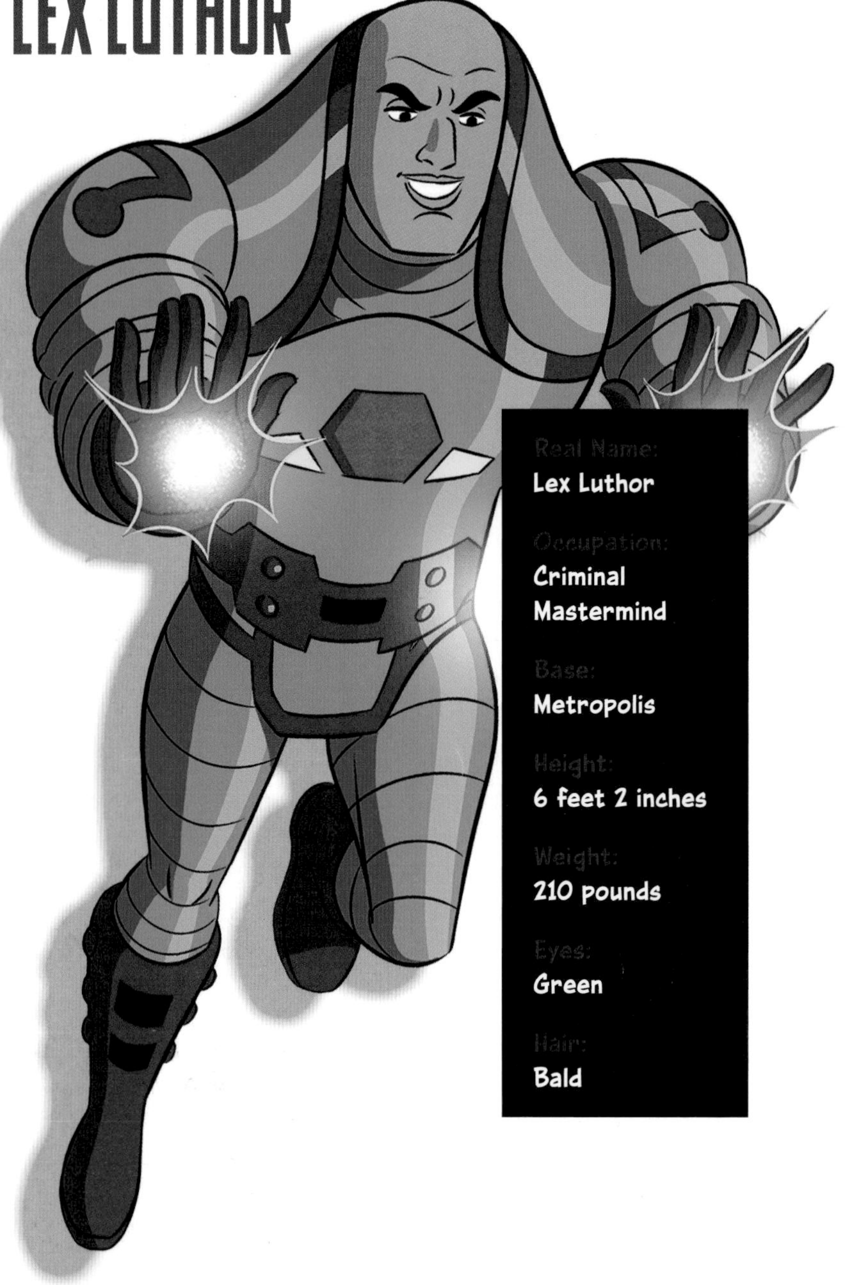

Real Name:
Lex Luthor

Occupation:
Criminal Mastermind

Base:
Metropolis

Height:
6 feet 2 inches

Weight:
210 pounds

Eyes:
Green

Hair:
Bald

Lex Luthor is one of the richest and most powerful people in Metropolis. He's known as a successful businessman to most, but Superman knows Lex's dirty secret — most of his wealth is ill-gotten, and behind the scenes he is a criminal mastermind. Superman as stopped many of Luthor's sinister schemes, but Lex is careful to never get caught red-handed. Lex wants to defeat or control Superman to strengthen his grip on Metropolis, but the Man of Steel is immune to Luthor's influence.

- Lex Luthor is a crafty businessman, but also a criminal mastermind. He has often enlisted the help of other super-villains in his criminal activities and to try to topple the Man of Steel.

- Lex has no superpowers of his own, but he is a scientific genius. He has developed several incredible inventions. These include his trademark armored battle suit, which gives him powers and abilities similar to the Man of Steel's.

- Luthor has gone to extreme lengths to defeat Superman. He transformed John Corben into a cybernetic monster! Lex failed to use the metal man, named Metallo, to bend the Man of Steel to his will. And when the villainess Livewire was short-circuited by Superman, it was Lex who shocked her back to life.

- In an attempt to become even more powerful, Lex once schemed his way into the office of President of the United States! It ended badly for him, however, when citizens discovered that he intentionally put the world at risk to increase his approval ratings.

YOU CHOOSE

SUPERMAN

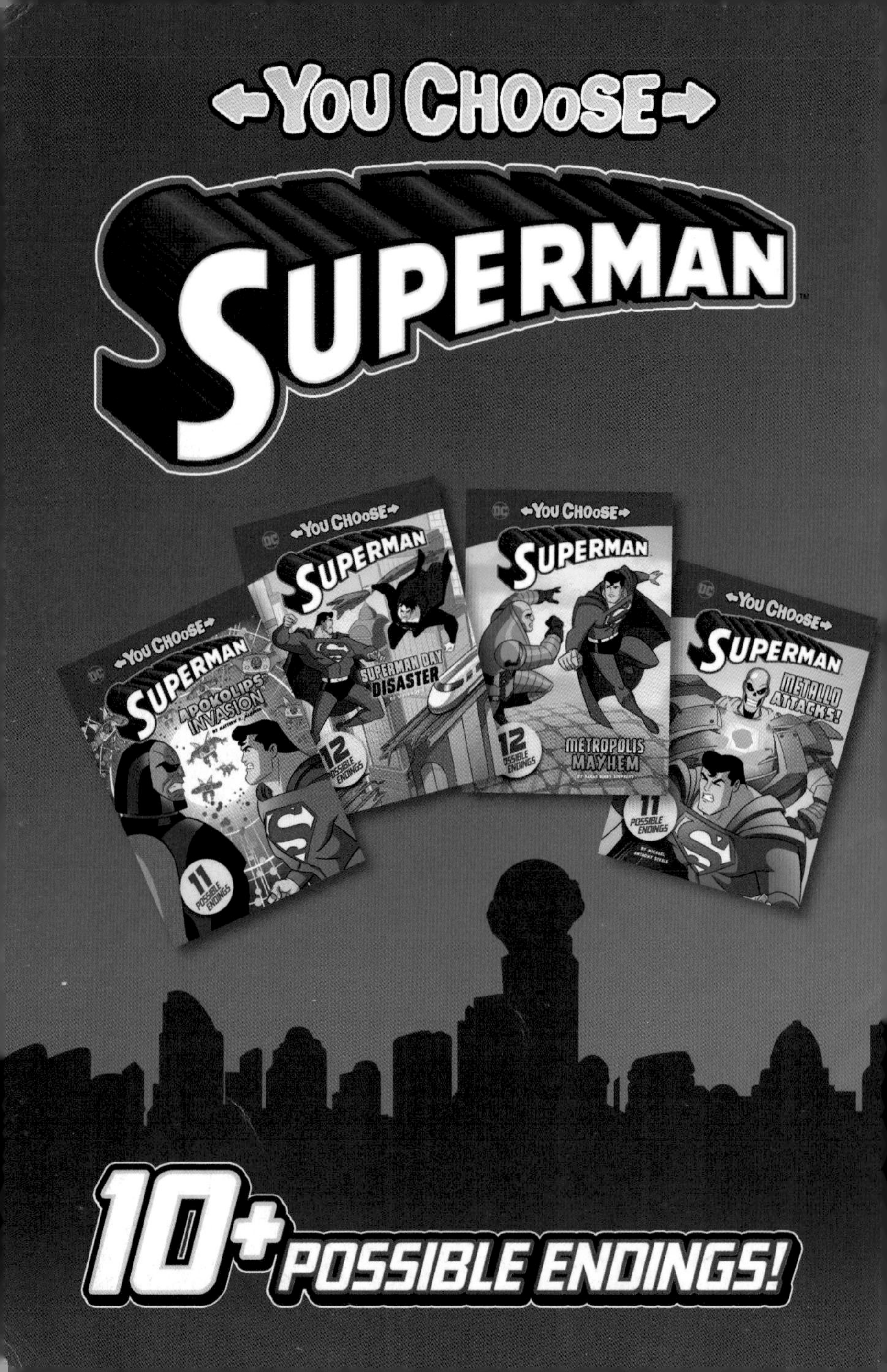
YOU CHOOSE
SUPERMAN
APOKOLIPS INVASION
11 POSSIBLE ENDINGS
YOU CHOOSE
SUPERMAN
SUPERMAN DAY DISASTER
12 POSSIBLE ENDINGS
YOU CHOOSE
SUPERMAN
12 POSSIBLE ENDINGS
METROPOLIS MAYHEM
YOU CHOOSE
SUPERMAN
METALLO ATTACKS!
11 POSSIBLE ENDINGS

10+ POSSIBLE ENDINGS!